He moved from the  move to the beat of th

'Come on,' he coaxed.

Baby looked at him and frowned, wrestling with herself. She loved the look of the dance, the *feel* of it when she watched the others, but could she do it? She hadn't expected her summer to start off like this. Had she only been here a few hours? There was something alluring and off limits about Johnny that she felt strangely attractive. He wasn't like the Neil Mumfords she usually went out with.

Finally, she moved toward him and started to sway with him, mirroring his steps. Johnny reached out and put his arm around her waist, bringing her closer.

'Stay loose,' he ordered.

'I am loose.'

'Come on, let go, stop holding on.'

Baby looked at him, suddenly drawn to him, to what he was willing her to do, to feel . . .

BABY, IT'S YOU

Baby, It's You

N.H. KLEINBAUM

Dirty Dancing ™

BANTAM BOOKS

TORONTO • NEW YORK • LONDON • SYDNEY • AUCKLAND

BABY, IT'S YOU
A BANTAM BOOK 0 553 401173

Originally published in Great Britain by Bantam Books

PRINTING HISTORY
Bantam edition published 1989

This book is set in 11 on 13 Palatino by Chippendale Type, Otley,
West Yorkshire.

Bantam Books are published by Transworld Publishers Ltd., 61–63
Uxbridge Road, Ealing, London W5 5SA, in Australia by Transworld
Publishers (Australia) Pty. Ltd., 15–23 Helles Avenue, Moorebank,
NSW 2170, and in New Zealand by Transworld Publishers (N.Z.)
Ltd., Cnr. Moselle and Waipareira Avenues, Henderson, Auckland.

Made and printed in Great Britain by
Cox & Wyman Ltd., Reading, Berks.

BABY, IT'S YOU

One

'Kellerman's Hotel, please.'

Eighteen-year-old Frances Kellerman shoved her overstuffed suitcase into the back seat of the yellow cab, slid into the seat and sighed.

'Boy it's hot,' she said, as she wiped beads of sweat from her forehead.

The driver nodded as the taxi careened out of the Monticello train station and onto the broad winding Route 17.

'So, you're going to Kellerman's?' the cabbie asked, chatting as he sped along the scenic highway lined with tall, green pine trees and an occasional billboard advertising one of the many mountain retreat hotels.

Frances nodded. 'My father owns the place,' she smiled. 'I'm going to work there for the summer.'

Baby stared out the window. She turned her head and smiled as she noticed a billboard for Kellerman's Mountain Retreat.

'Nice place,' he said. 'The wife and me went there once for an anniversary. Nice place. Real classy! So your old man runs the place. Pretty nice! I think I remember meeting him. Tall guy, kind of balding. A real *kibbitzer*, always telling jokes.'

Frances nodded again, then she smiled and closed her eyes. She hoped to silence the talkative driver and cursed herself for having started the conversation in the first place.

Kellerman's! It was more than her own last name, it was a piece of her family history. She remembered the stories she'd heard repeated with pride about her grandfather who'd started the place decades ago as a small group of cabins. Then it was turned over to her Uncle Jake who expanded it and made it a successful, popular resort, especially for people from New York City. Now it was her own father, Max Kellerman, who ran it, after abandoning the insurance business. Uncle Jake and Aunt Sylvia were on the other side of the resort business now as residents of a "Swinging" senior citizens condominium complex in Scottsdale, Arizona.

As she relaxed with her head back against the sticky vinyl seat of the cab, the hotel flashed before her eyes. She saw her mother and father sitting on the huge, wooden lawn chairs watching as she and her sister, Lisa, played on the special double red swings.

Mother and father. They were together, then, seemingly happy. Life had been simple then back in the '50s.

But now it was 1963 and nothing was simple anymore. The '50s was when they called her "Baby", instead of Frances, and she didn't mind. Before the excitement of President Kennedy and the dramatic inspiration of Dr Martin Luther King. Before she decided that she wanted more than Kellerman's Hotel and planned to go into the Peace Corps. That was then. When she thought no one in the world was as wonderful or as perfect as her father.

The taxi jerked suddenly, she straightened up and opened her eyes.

But now that they were divorced Mom was alone in their old sprawling house in Roslyn on Long Island, and Dad had Kellerman's, way up here in the Catskill Mountains. Had it really been three years since she'd seen her own father? she thought, nervously anticipating the reunion.

Daddy, Daddy, how could you? She'd wondered how and why ever since she'd learned the truth. She still resented his infidelity. How he had hurt her mother who had always been there for him and everyone. The story was a familiar one. It sounded like a B-rated movie. Her father had run off with a young secretary. Of course that didn't last. But, then, neither did the marriage of twenty years.

Her older sister Lisa's reaction bothered Frances, even though she realized it was typical of Lisa.

'Baby,' she'd said nonchalantly. 'Marriage is almost Neanderthal these days. Mom and Dad are just typical of the times. Divorce is in. Free love is where it's at.'

Lisa was so dumb and selfish sometimes, Frances thought. Now she was going to see her father and she wanted it to be a good summer. Only a month ago, her friend Monica's father, who was even younger than Max, had died suddenly. Monica was still in shock and grief. There wasn't much she was able to do for her friend except be there for her and listen to her memories.

It made Frances feel that life was too short to let her anger continue to seethe and keep her apart from her own father. Here she was on her way to her father's hotel for the summer, hopefully to mend fences, get a great suntan, and maybe, if she didn't try too hard, to fall in love.

In their brief conversation her father promised that she could work at the hotel, maybe as a

waitress or camp counselor. She didn't want to
be treated like the owner's daughter. Just because
she was, she knew she'd make sure he treated
her the same as everyone else working there.

The taxi driver screeched on the brakes and
turned up the familiar wide curving road leading
to the beautiful stone and brick main house
which Uncle Jake had built. It was just as she
remembered it. A wide new welcoming porch
had been added to the front of the building.
Rows of wooden rocking chairs and love seats
were scattered on the porch, many already occu-
pied by talkative, smiling guests.

The manicured lawn surrounding the main
house led to the huge golf course in the distance.
In front of the building still stood the old familiar
double swing.

She opened the door of the cab, got out and
stretched. She looked around and took a long,
deep breath of the clean mountain air. The
cabbie put her luggage on the ground. He told
her the meter fare and smiled as he looked
around admiringly at the hotel.

'So have a good summer. Maybe the wife and
I will come up for a weekend and see you
around,' the driver said, as she paid him.

'Great! Do that. I know if you stay here you'll
have a wonderful time.'

The cab pulled away and Frances stood looking around at the countryside. In the distance she heard announcements on the loudspeakers. She tried to make out exactly what was being said. Something about shuffleboard and ping-pong. Simon Sez would be played at the pool at 5 p.m.

'Just like old times.' She shook her head slowly and realized she was grinning. Frances turned as the sound of hot Latin music came rushing out of the dance room, drowning out the rest of the announcements.

'The old biddies must be getting their dancing lessons,' Baby thought as a tall, skinny disheveled bellhop suddenly appeared and grabbed her bag.

'Sorry I wasn't here to help you out of your car,' he apologized. 'Welcome to Kellerman's. Where a weekend feels like a lifetime.'

She looked at the bellhop in amazement and laughed out loud.

'Sorry, I don't wanna make it seem like you're doing time on Devil's Island,' he laughed. 'It's just that three days here are so great . . . ' He stopped and looked at her, suddenly smitten by her beautiful blue eyes and open laugh. 'I'm Norman. I'll check you in.'

'Thanks Norman,' she smiled. 'I think I'll just walk around. See you later.'

Frances walked along the crisply cut grass toward the sound of the music that had attracted her attention before. She walked toward the ballroom rehearsal hall where the sound grew louder. Standing by the door, she peered in at two young dancers, engrossed in a hot and sexy dance, one she'd never seen before.

She guessed both the guy and the girl were in their twenties, tough and sexy. They were dancing together in slow, exaggerated movements, hips curling, lost in the music. Their bodies looked sultry, yet their facial expressions were tough.

Baby watched for a minute and left quickly, but without being seen. She felt that she had intruded on a private moment.

She walked from the ballroom to the other side of the grounds and stood at a wooden railing watching the activity of people at play. The hotel was alive with games of badminton, horseshoes, canoeing on the lake below, and the inevitable country favorite, Simon Sez.

Baby watched families at the pool and smiled at the applause for a slightly overweight boy who did a cannonball dive into twelve feet of water. She noticed a heavyset man wearing a terrycloth robe lounging with a sun reflector to his face, listening to his wife who was painting red nail polish on her toes and complaining about how she had eaten too much for breakfast when she'd promised herself she would diet.

'Nothing changes at Kellerman's,' Baby said out loud. 'It's just the way it used to be!'

Suddenly she heard her father's voice over the loudspeaker system: 'For all you rock 'n' roll fans who love juggling, our own Lucille Snyder will sing *Twist and Shout*, while hula-hooping her way into your hearts. That's in the card room in five minutes!'

Inside the bar, Max Kellerman finished his announcements as the intercom buzzed.

'Get that, Harry,' he asked the bartender.

'Max,' the bartender called. 'You forgot we have arts and crafts in the card room.'

'Put them in the sun room, move Herbie's puppet show in to the gazebo, and have Paula's make-up class at the lake,' Max orchestrated as he puffed on a huge cigar.

Returning to the microphone, he bellowed, 'And, folks, let's not forget tonight is movie night . . . *"Lawrence of Arabia!"'*

Baby walked back toward the main house heading toward the sound of her father's voice. She again cut through the ballroom rehearsal hall where the sound of the Latin music was still throbbing.

The dancers were now giving a mambo lesson to a group of middle-aged suburbanites. Baby walked in and stopped for a minute, watching the lesson. As the music ended, the good-looking guy spotted her.

She eyed him quickly and felt her heart pounding. He was tall and slim with dark brown hair and piercing blue eyes which twinkled impishly as he approached her. His slim hips swayed gracefully even as he walked toward her.

'You here for the class?'

'No. I'm looking for . . . '

'The card room? Ping-pong? Mahjong?' he interrupted, mockingly.

'Mr Kellerman,' Baby said.

'Lucky guy,' he replied, taking in Baby's slim frame and full lips with his eyes.

'Mr Kellerman,' he said, as Max approached from behind. 'There's a lovely lady looking for you.'

Frances turned. Her father had put on some weight and was grayer around the temples but he was still a tall, handsome figure of a man.

'What lovely lady!' Max boomed as he opened his arms wide. 'That's my Baby!'

'Hi, Dad.'

Max grinned, ran up and swept Frances into his arms.

'It's good to see you! But you weren't supposed to be here till two.' He hugged her as the group watched. Turning, Max said, 'Johnny Castle,

Penny Lopez, everyone, I'd like you to meet my daughter, Baby.'

'It's Frances,' Baby corrected.

'What Frances! You're my Baby. And folks, this is some gal I have here. She's going to Mount Holyoke College in September. Graduated top in her class at Roslyn High . . . '

'Dad, please,' Frances said, begging him with her eyes to stop bragging in front of these strangers.

'What? What?' Max asked in surprise. 'I'm just telling the facts here. Oh, Johnny,' he said, turning to the handsome dancer, 'there's one little thing. Baby wants to work this summer, believe it or not. I told her she doesn't have to, but she's insisted. So I was thinking she could take over as talent coordinator.'

'That's . . . one *little* thing?' Johnny bristled.

'You've got enough to do teaching the mambo to our wonderful guests here,' Max said.

'Baby can work on something special with you for this coming Sunday. You know we're having Miss Subways up here and I want everything to be perfect.'

'I thought I was handling it,' Johnny said angrily.

'Well, no, it's off your hands,' Max answered, obviously unconcerned by Johnny's angry tone.

Baby looked at Johnny and gulped. 'Look,

Dad, I could be a waitress or a . . . '

Max laughed. 'A waitress? My daughter? This job's perfect for you . . . You just put together the entertainment. Johnny'll brief you later.'

Max put his arm around his daughter and led her out of the ballroom. 'Right now, I want to hear about what you've been up to . . . how you got to be so grown-up all of a sudden.

'And you can tell me about your sister, too. I guess she's really grown up now. That Lisa, what a gypsy. I haven't heard from her in ages!'

'That's usually what happens when you become eighteen, Dad,' she shrugged. 'Lisa's off in Paris painting or something. You know Lisa. Free spirit of the '60s!'

Max put his arm around his daughter's shoulder, and as Max walked her out of the door, Penny and Johnny stared after Baby.

'One little thing, huh?' Penny asked grimly, shaking her raven black hair angrily.

Johnny took a deep breath. 'Forget it. Let's get back to work. That stupid Miss Subways visit isn't worth my time thinking about.' He took a moment to collect himself, then turned back to the waiting guests.

'Sorry for the interruption, folks, but when the boss comes in . . . you know. Let's get back to that mambo!'

*   *   *

Max and Baby crossed the grounds, passing guests working on their suntans and others napping under the tall green trees.

'Dad, when I said I wanted a job, I meant any job, no special treatment,' Frances protested. 'I think that guy Johnny was upset . . . '

'What special?' Max asked. 'Who knows more about talent than you? All those years of ballet . . '

'I quit ballet when I was eight, Dad.'

'So don't do anything,' Max said. 'Let's just spend the summer catching up. Your mom's kept you to herself long enough.'

'She didn't keep me, Dad. I didn't want to come till now. And I guess you felt . . . too guilty to spend much time with us.'

'Guilty? Who told you I felt . . . ' Max took a deep breath. 'You know, maybe it wasn't all my fault . . . your mother and me breaking up. Maybe you're old enough now to hear *my* side of the story.'

'Go ahead,' Baby urged, stopping in her tracks. 'I'd like to.'

Max winced. 'You want to talk about it now?'

'Sure,' Baby said. 'We may as well start sometime. Let's get off to a clean start.'

'How about later?' Max suggested, looking out across the lawn. 'Over lunch? Oh, I forgot, I told your favourite cousin, Robin, you'd have lunch with her and look—,' he smiled, pointing with relief— 'there she is!'

Baby turned and saw her younger cousin, Robin, a robust and jolly girl, moaning and panting on the tennis court as she vainly attempted a volley.

Max ran over to the court, pulling Baby by the hand.

'Robin!' he called. 'Look who's here!'

Robin waved. 'Hi, Bab—' she called out, and then was cut off and silenced as a tennis ball slammed her in the stomach.

'She's so glad you're here,' Max said to Baby. 'I've even arranged for the two of you to room together.'

Baby moaned. She'd left a wonderful room of her own in Roslyn, to have to share a cabin with her nosy, boy-crazy cousin Robin! They hardly knew each other! It had been years since they'd been friends.

Now they were . . . different. Spending the summer with Robin was *definitely not* what Baby had in mind. 'Oh no, Dad, not that! Couldn't I just camp out? Take a linen closet?' But Max didn't even hear as he led Baby along the side of one tennis court to another.

'Now here's someone I really want you to meet . . . Neil, come over here!' Max called.

Baby tried to hide her embarrassment as she watched a clean-cut, but, to her mind, only blandly good-looking guy of about twenty-one, appear instantly at Max's side.

'Neil Mumford, this is Baby. My daughter. The one I was telling you all about.'

'Hi,' Neil smiled.

'Hello,' Baby said, annoyed by her father's manipulation.

'Neil's doing a stint here as a lifeguard before he goes to med school this fall. I thought you two should get to know each other . . . maybe at the supper dance tonight.'

Neil smiled. 'Fine with me,' he said to Max. Turning to Baby, he added, 'Pick you up around eight, OK?'

'Perfect,' Max said, before Baby could answer.

'See you then,' Neil smiled and walked away.

Baby turned to Max, her nostrils flaring. 'Dad, what are you doing?'

'What do you mean what am I doing? I was just—'

'You were setting me up with some med student so I don't run away with a Rumanian bus boy!'

'Just make sure you get your shots before you go,' Max laughed.

Baby smiled. 'Dad, you don't have to take care of me anymore.'

'Who's taking care of you? I was just . . . '

'Making her crazy before she's unpacked one bag,' a husky, warm Southern voice finished the sentence.

They turned to see Sweets Walker coming up behind them.

'Hi, Sweets,' Baby smiled, reaching out to give a warm hug to an old friend. 'I'm glad to see you again.'

Taking her hand, he crooned, 'Long time, no see . . . You're all grown-up now. We missed you here.'

'Me too.' She squeezed the black piano player, a man as sweet as his name, who had been at Kellerman's every summer for as long as she could remember.

She glanced at Max and then turned back to Sweets. 'It took me a while to realize people aren't perfect, that's all,' she said.

'Who's not perfect?' Max looked aghast. 'You don't think I'm—?'

'I think you're the only dad I've got . . . and I don't want to lose you again.'

She hugged them both.

'Well, I better get to work. Don't want the boss to give me a hard time!' Frances smiled at her father.

'Good luck,' Max said. 'Oh listen . . . I want you to fill me in on this new dance routine

Johnny's worked up for Saturday night. Every time I ask to see it, he says he needs "artistic autonomy". I didn't think he knew a word that long!' Max laughed.

Frances scowled. 'So you want me to spy for you . . . '

'I didn't say that.' He looked at Sweets. 'Did I say . . . ?'

'I'd better grab a clipboard . . . make them think I know what I'm doing. I haven't even been to my room yet, but I can take care of unpacking later. I've only been here one hour and I already have two outrageous assignments: spy for Dad and create a sensational show for Miss Subways! Honestly! This is going to be some summer! See ya!'

Baby grinned and dashed off.

'She's turned into quite a woman,' Sweets said to Max, smiling as Baby headed toward the ballroom.

'You know what, Sweets?' Max said. 'I think I liked it better when she was twelve.'

Two

Baby ran up the steps into the rehearsal hall, clutching a clipboard for security.

'Here goes, day one of my summer job,' she thought, as she entered the ballroom where a group of young staff members was assembled. They eyed Baby warily. Baby noticed that most were in their early twenties; the girls were dressed in tight pants or short shorts and halter tops, and the guys wore cut-offs or tight jeans and tee-shirts.

They focused on Baby as she tried to organize the gathering.

'So . . . I was hoping Johnny would've briefed me before this rehearsal,' she said.

'Unfortunately, I didn't know there was a rehearsal till Norman told me.' She glanced at Johnny who looked around nonchalantly.

'G'head, brief her,' one of the dancers said to Johnny. 'But make it brief, man!'

The group laughed. Baby flushed with discomfort.

'OK,' Johnny said, turning to Baby. 'Our first big show's Saturday night. Your father got Jack Lacey to headline. I lined up Norman here to do his stand-up routine. Sweets has his number with the band. That's it.'

'I hear there's also a dance routine,' Baby said.

Johnny nodded. 'That was going to be a surprise . . . A little something extra.'

'Why don't we start with that?' Baby suggested.

'It's fine. It's under control,' Johnny said flatly.

'Look, I'm on your side,' Baby said, trying to break through the ice. 'I love dance. It's one of the reasons my father gave me this job.'

'Is that so?' Johnny said.

'I took ballet lessons when I was a kid.'

'Ballet?' Johnny nodded, smirking. 'No kidding?'

'I mean, I was never in *Swan Lake* or anything,' Baby stammered. 'But I've always been a fan of dance. Dancers.'

'All right, then, why don't you get in the back row?' Johnny smiled.

'What?'

'Everyone in the staff with any talent is in it . . . that should include you.'

'I know, I just . . . '

'I'm sure you won't have any trouble following along,' Johnny said. 'What with your training and all.'

Baby looked around at the group. She felt their wariness as they stared back at her, serious and unfriendly. Penny leaned on Johnny's shoulder and smirked broadly.

'I really can't,' Baby said, afraid she was going to cry. 'I mean, I haven't danced in . . . '

'What's your problem?' Johnny asked. 'I thought you were on our side!'

Baby stood silently, immobile. She felt the challenge in his eyes.

'OK,' Johnny continued, breaking up the group, 'make room for one more in the back row . . . and *let's do it*!'

Baby looked at him, took a deep breath and walked to the back row. Johnny put on the music, the same Latin soul she had seen him dance to earlier. The group started to dance, capturing the beat and rhythm of the sound. Baby watched for a moment, overwhelmed by the steps, the rhythm, the heated energy around her. She made a small attempt to follow along, tripping over her feet, turning in the wrong direction and not knowing when to turn, bend or jump.

After a few humiliating minutes, she stopped and slid to the side of the room, as the pulse and the dancers continued. She caught Johnny's eyes and quickly looked away, angry and humiliated.

Baby ducked out the side door as the dancers pulsated. The sound of the music rang in her ears, her head ached. She couldn't tell if it was from the music or the anger she felt.

They wouldn't even give her a chance, she knew that now. She was the boss's daughter.

Baby walked aimlessly around the grounds trying to get under control.

'This is my first day. I'm not going to let them spoil my entire summer. Who does that guy think he is anyway?'

Baby's mind raced, confused and frustrated by the new sensations she was feeling toward this stranger. Johnny had embarrassed her, made her feel miserable and worthless, and yet, something about him caused her heart to pound.

'I can't be attracted to him! I don't even know him,' she said to herself as she walked aimlessly around the grounds for an hour after the disastrous scene, trying to get her emotions under control.

She headed toward the staff quarters, which were set deep in the woods, away from the main house.

Still clenching her clipboard, Baby walked across the small wooden bridge that led to a flight of steps up a to a row of wooden cabins where most of the staff lived. Since her father said she would be rooming with Robin she wouldn't even have a chance to make friends with the staff by living here.

She reached the top of the steps and walked toward a gravelly path where she spotted Johnny and a group of the dancers who had been at the rehearsal.

Johnny was bent over the open hood of his shiny red Chevy, tinkering with the engine. Penny stood next to him, wearing turquoise toreador pants and a black halter top, holding some tools. Music blasted from a transistor radio perched on the hood. Several staff members leaned against the car, singing, clapping and shaking to the music as Baby walked up.

'Could I talk to you?' she asked Johnny.

Johnny stood up and looked her in the eyes. 'Sure . . . shoot.'

He kept his eyes on her, waiting. Baby glanced at Penny, feeling uneasy.

'I think it was very unfair of you to . . . ' Baby began.

'What *is* fair?' Penny interrupted. 'You taking his job away?'

'Look, if it's making everyone that unhappy . . . ' Baby said.

'Don't sweat it,' Johnny said, wiping off a

wrench. 'We're cool.'

'Who's cool?' Penny asked, her dark eyes flaring.

Johnny turned to Penny and grabbed her by the arm. 'Her father hears anyone's making *her* miserable this summer, they're out . . . dig?'

'Maybe it's not worth it,' Penny said. 'Maybe we should get out.'

'And do what?' Johnny asked her.

Penny threw down the tools. 'Never mind. Forget it,' she said. 'Let's split,' she said to the others, who followed her toward the cabins.

'Hey, duchess,' Johnny called. 'Wait a minute.'

Johnny sighed as Penny stalked off, ignoring him.

Baby looked at Johnny. 'Look, I really don't want to cause any . . . '

'Problem is, you can't see it from where you are,' he said, not giving her a chance to finish. 'Penny, she checks out groceries all winter for people like you. Me, I'm a mechanic, like my old man. We fix your cars.'

'I'm sorry,' Baby said, embarrassed by the conversation. 'I didn't mean to . . . '

'The summers are a chance for us . . . For you, it's a vacation. A little fun job on the side.'

Baby stiffened. 'I take this job very seriously. That's why I don't like being humiliated in front of all those . . . '

'Hey!' Johnny interrupted. 'It bothers you so much, learn the routine.'

'I told you, I haven't danced in . . . '

'Look, you think the rest of them are dancers? They can move. They wanted something more. I made them move together – so they're dancers.'

Johnny stared out at the countryside and took a long breath. 'Look, no one could've done what I asked you to do today. I'm sorry I did that to you. You have to know the basics. Come on, I'll show you.'

He moved from the car and stood beside her, starting to move to the beat of the music on the transistor radio.

'Come on,' he coaxed. 'Do what I do.'

Baby looked at him and frowned, wrestling with herself. She loved the look of the dance, the *feel* of it when she watched the others, but could she do it? She hadn't expected her summer to start off like this. Had she only been here a few hours? There was something alluring and off limits about Johnny that she felt strangely attractive. He wasn't like the Neil Mumfords she usually went out with.

Finally, she moved toward him and started to sway with him, mirroring his steps. Johnny reached out and put his arm around her waist, bringing her closer.

'Stay loose,' he ordered.

'I am loose.'

'Come on, let go, stop holding on.'

Baby looked at him, suddenly drawn to him, to what he was willing her to do, to feel. Then instinctively, she clenched and backed away.

'I'm going to be late . . . ' she stammered. 'For the supper dance.'

Johnny stopped and gave a small wry smile. 'Wouldn't want to miss that.'

Baby turned to go and then looked back to Johnny. 'Why do you make me feel so . . . stupid?' she asked.

'Maybe I'm just too dim to carry on a conversation with the boss's daughter,' he said.

'No, that's not it,' she said, shaking her head. 'Why do people think they know everything about someone, what kind of person they really are, without – when they don't even give them a chance to . . . '

Baby trailed off, angry and exasperated, unable to say anything more. She turned and ran down the steps and across the bridge to get ready for the dance her father had arranged for her to attend with Neil.

Johnny's eyes followed Baby as she ran away from him.

Three

'I'm so glad you're here. You know, I've been coming up here every summer, even after my folks turned the place over to your dad,' Robin said, as she clipped beer-can rollers into her hair.

'I figured my social life would get better with Uncle Max around instead of my mother. I couldn't stand the thought of being at that retirement condo in Arizona with my parents. It's like a sauna there in the summer.'

Robin looked into the mirror, frowned and pulled open a tube of Clerasil.

'Darn zits!' she scowled as she rubbed the cream over a small pimple on her face.

'Not that I *have* a social life,' Robin continued, as Baby stood absolutely silent, staring into space, not really hearing a word Robin said. She couldn't help thinking about Johnny. She tried to push the feeling of being held by him and the rhythm of the dance out of her head.

'So far the highlight of *this* week was when I sat down on some guy in musical chairs,' Robin continued. 'I was "out", of course, so I didn't get to know him very well. I'm going to die if I don't meet someone soon!' she wailed.

Robin plopped onto her bed and stared at Baby. 'Are you going to be a virgin when you're married?' she asked.

'What?' Baby snapped back from her daydreams. 'No. Yes. What was the question?'

'I said, are you going to be a virgin when you're married?'

Baby shrugged. 'I don't know.'

'You don't know?' Robin looked incredulous. Her eyes narrowed. 'You're one now, aren't you?'

'Yes, I guess. I mean, I am.'

'Baby,' Robin said, moving off her bed and closer to Baby's suitcase. 'I know that you've only been here two days, but we're cousins and roommates. Are you hiding something from me?'

'No. I'm just thinking.'

'About what? A boy?' Robin asked excitedly. 'You can tell me. My lips are sealed. It's Neil, isn't it? I saw you two at the supper dance. Oh Baby, he's a vision – those teeth, that tan, the entire physique! And a life guard and a med student to boot! The catch of the summer and you've *got* him!'

'Who?' Baby looked confused.

'I want to know everything,' Robin said, ignoring the question. 'Is he a good kisser? Did you get that melty feeling when he did it, or did you just panic and palpitate? Was he slow and romantic or hot and fiery? Do you love him?'

Baby focused on Robin. 'What *are* you talking about?'

'You and Neil, of course,' Robin said, looking annoyed yet daydreamy.

'Robin, I just met him. And besides, he's not for me. He's not my type. Too blonde or something. Too into himself for my taste. Why don't you try for him?'

'Mmmm, do you think so?' Robin sighed thoughtfully. 'Well, I know you're thinking about someone. I'm never wrong when it comes to boys. You think Neil might . . . ' she asked herself as she looked into the mirror again, grabbed a jar of cold cream, and started stroking some thoughtfully on her face.

Baby didn't answer. Mechanically she took her clothes out of the suitcase and folded them on the bed as she daydreamed about her dance with Johnny.

'Hey, it's late, Robin. I don't want to talk now.

But honest, you should go after Neil if you think
he's such a hunk. G'night!'

The next day Norman was rehearsing on the
ballroom stage as a group of dancers sat in the
audience along with Johnny and Baby. Baby
watched horrified, clutching her clipboard.

'So I was walking down the street and this
bum, this cop, this—' Norman sputtered as he
tried to put together a joke for his stand-up
comedy routine.

Baby moved from her chair next to Johnny as
she watched Norman struggling.

'What is he doing up there?' she whispered to
Johnny.

'He'll have it by Saturday,' Johnny assured
her.

'What?' Baby asked. 'A nervous breakdown?
He's going to make us all look like idiots. We've
got to replace him.'

Johnny turned angrily to Baby. 'What if he's
not afraid of looking like an idiot. What if he's
willing to take that chance?'

'What does that have to do with . . . '

Johnny interrupted her. 'You think Gleason or
Benny started out with more than a hope, a
dream? So he's not ready for the Ed Sullivan
Show. You step on that dream now – he'll *never*
be ready! He needs a little encouragement, that's

all. But, hey, you're the one with the clipboard –
it's up to you.'

Baby frowned. 'I know, I just . . . I . . . ' She
turned away and focused back on Norman on
stage.

'I got them from a joke magazine, two bucks,
two thousand jokes,' Norman apologized as he
stood before the group. 'I was going to do some
stuff about my father and his fish store, how my
mom put lemons in his shower nozzle but . . . '

'But what?' Baby asked. 'Now, that's funny.'

'It is?' Norman hopped off the stage and
walked toward Baby.

'Johnny, why don't you run through the
dance,' Baby said. 'I'll work with Norman.' She
put her arm through his and led him to a table in
the corner.

Johnny smiled. 'You got it, boss. OK, dancers
let's get to it *now*!'

The kids jumped from their seats onto the
stage and began the dance routine. A few
moments later, Max walked quietly in and sat
unnoticed, in the back.

The dancers jumped and jiggled to the heated
rhythm. As Johnny turned, he suddenly spotted
Max.

'Okay, hold it right there,' he called hastily to
the group.

'Please,' Max said, walking out into the light,

'don't stop on my account.'

'We're really not ready for visitors yet, Mr Kellerman,' Johnny said,

'That's all right, I think I've seen enough!' Max said testily. 'Baby,' he shouted, 'may I have a word with you?'

Baby's eyes caught Johnny's and she took a deep breath, gearing herself for a confrontation with her father. She walked to the side of the room with Max out of earshot of the group.

'Why didn't you tell me he was doing this . . . this . . . what is it anyway? Last summer he just did fancy foxtrots!'

Baby looked at her father. 'You didn't like it, huh?' she asked, knowing the answer before she heard it.

'It's an insult to the eyes, ears, and forget the intelligence!' Max hissed. 'I should have cut it out as soon as he handed me that "artistic autonomy" bull stuff.'

'Well now I have the "artistic autonomy", Dad, and I don't want to cut it. It's different. It's exciting. It's *fun!*'

She watched Max bristle but continued before he could cut her off. 'Dad, how much Simon Sez can you shove down people's throats? The dance is great! Take it from someone with years of ballet behind her. You're making this place much more exciting than when Uncle Jake

ran it. Saturday night you'll have an exciting
dance show and Sunday you're honoring Miss
Subway of the Month! Dad, this is great stuff!
You're putting your *own* mark on the Kellerman
tradition!'

Max sighed, shaking his head in defeat. 'I
should've put you to work in the laundry room,'
he laughed.

Baby hugged him and ran back to the group.
Max lingered in the ballroom, still unsettled by
the outcome. Baby turned and stared at him,
eyeing the door. He finally shook his head one
final time and walked out.

The kids gathered around Baby, waiting. She
turned to Johnny.

'He liked it,' she smiled.

Johnny held her gaze. His face slowly opened
into a warm and grateful smile. He turned to the
group, raised his hands in victory and shouted,
'OK! Let's get back to work!'

The dancers cheered and scrambled back on
stage.

Later that night, Johnny sat on his bed pulling
on a black sock singing *Bring It On Home To Me*
along with Sam Cooke. The door swung open
and Penny stalked angrily in, scratching the
needle across the record and turning off the
machine.

'You got something against Sam Cooke?' Johnny asked, as he stood up to put the music back on.

'I got something against what's going on with you and Miss Hotshot College Queen,' Penny said, eyeing him irately.

Johnny looked surprised. 'What're you talking about?'

'The two of you looked like Ozzie and Harriet, running the show today,' she said.

Johnny flashed a toothy grin. 'Oh yeah? You think she turns me on, huh? You think we discuss Greek philosophy together or somethin'?' He chuckled and finished putting on his sock.

'I just don't like you kissing up to the boss's daughter. 'Cause remember, when she goes back to college, you go back to . . . '

Johnny's face darkened. 'I know what I go back to. I don't need you to remind me, OK?'

He turned and stared out the window for a moment.

'Look, all I know is, if she's happy, her old man's happy. He's letting us do the routine, isn't he?'

Penny's face brightened with sudden understanding. 'Oh, so that's why you've been so nice to her? That's why you . . . ?'

Johnny pulled her close to him, fingering her lips.

'Come on,' he smiled. 'Lemme remember how pretty that mouth is when it's not asking so many questions.'

Penny smiled broadly. 'My pleasure,' she said, pulling him closer to a kiss.

Down the path near the staff cabins, Baby and Robin stood outside the doorway of the staff dance room. Baby had tried to convince Robin to come to the staff party. Now, as they were close enough to the cabin to hear the pounding music, Robin was still resisting and complaining.

'Baby, you cannot do this,' Robin whined. 'I won't let you!'

'Why not?' Baby said. 'I was invited. Norman invited me.'

Robin pulled her away from the door. 'Will you just come with me to charades in the main social hall and act like a normal person?'

Baby looked toward the doorway. 'Robin, I don't know if I want to be a normal person anymore,' she said longingly.

'What do you want to do, go in there and eat a marijuana cookie?' Robin said. 'Those people are not like you or me. We don't belong in there. You know that!'

'All they do is dance, Robin. Norman told me. They do it almost every night. Besides, even though I don't live on this side, I'm still a member of the staff.'

'This is ridiculous,' Robin said angrily. 'You're acting ridiculous. Your father owns this place! How do you know they don't wind up having an orgy?'

Baby shook her head in disgust.

'Baby, I just told you, they're not like us. They're not our . . . group.'

'What's so great about *our* group?' Baby asked, turning to her cousin.

'Listen to me,' Robin said. 'Their parents are bus drivers, delivery men. I bet some of their fathers are unemployed, living on welfare even, who knows?'

Baby's face reddened. 'Look Robin,' she said angrily, 'my father cheated on my mother, yours cheats at cards.'

'What does that have to . . . ' Robin looked confused.

'Robin, go play charades. Give the other team *Return to Peyton Place*, be a real wild woman,' Baby said walking toward the door. 'See you later.'

She smiled, turned and headed into the staff dance. Robin stared after her in disbelief.

The dance room was hot and smoky. Baby

sidled in, staying close to the wall, her eyes wide with excitement, almost embarrassment, as she watched the dancing gyrations.

'Wow,' she thought. 'to be able to do that with your body with someone like . . . ' She spotted Johnny dancing in the crowd. He turned and saw her.

When the record ended, he walked over to Baby.

'I saw what you did for Norman during rehearsal,' Johnny said. He really is a funny guy. With the right kind of help and encouragement like you gave him, he might be a real comedian some day. It was great the way to tell him how to stand up, how to use his hands and body and use the jokes that he could relate to rather than the ones from a magazine. Anyhow, I know he appreciated your attention and interest. It was a nice thing to do.'

'For the boss's daughter,' she jibbed.

'Especially for the boss's daughter,' he smiled. 'Why won't you dance with me? Don't you trust me? 'Fraid I'm gonna make you look bad?'

Baby shook her head. 'No, no, that's not it.'

'Good,' he said, smiling and taking her hand. 'Well, let's dance.'

Johnny swept Baby up in his arms, so unexpectedly she practically swooned. The beat of the music bounced off the walls as Baby and

Johnny danced. She followed his every move,
laughing, her eyes bright with excitement, her
heart beating loudly, as he twisted and swirled
her around.

'Do this,' he instructed, showing her a sexy
move of his hips.

She palpitated as he watched, trying to imitate.

'No, this way,' he said, putting his hands on
her hips to guide her.

Baby closed her eyes as she felt her hips move
to his rhythm, losing herself in the music, relaxed
and released by the heat, the smell and the
sound.

As she gyrated, lost in the rhythm, Johnny
playfully let go of her hand and grabbed Penny
to dance, leaving Baby dancing by herself.

Caught up in the music, it was a moment
before she realized she was dancing alone. Her
heart pounding, her face flushed, she slowly
made her way off the floor and out the door as
Johnny and Penny continued to dance.

Maybe Robin was right, she thought as she
rushed back to her room, glad to leave the
pulsating music behind her but unable to stop
her own racing heart.

Four

The next morning, as experienced waiters and waitresses swiftly carried trays of food from the dining room to the pool area, Baby precariously made her way along the path, balancing a tray stacked with breakfast orders.

Johnny, Penny and Sweets sat together at a poolside table, watching intently as she emerged in her new waitress uniform.

'You think the old man's gonna buy that this was all her idea?' Penny asked Johnny, as Baby carefully placed the tray on the cart and started handing plates of food to the guests at a nearby table.

'She told me this morning she decided she was going to tell him she didn't want the hassle of running the show,' Johnny said. 'She just wants to be in it.'

'But the old man likes the dance,' Penny said. 'We don't need her anymore.'

Johnny's eyes followed Baby's slim figure in

the starched black uniform with white apron and collar. 'She's part of the staff, for real now. She wants in, she should be in,' he said flatly.

Penny glared at him, not missing the fact that his eyes hadn't moved from Baby as she darted around the patio. Baby headed back to the dining room, and Penny turned her icy gaze toward her.

'Excuse me,' Baby said to a guest, as she passed with a tray.

Before she reached the dining room, she felt someone grab her arm.

'Robin! Watch it! I'll drop the tray!'

Robin pulled her into the dining room, behind a potted plant. Baby blinked and squinted, trying to adjust her eyes from the glare of the sunlit patio to the comparative darkness of the dining room. 'Someone dared you, didn't they?' Robin insisted. 'They dared you to dress up like this and . . . '

Baby gently pushed Robin away. 'Look, I'm busy now, Robin,' she smiled and started to walk toward the kitchen.

'Something happened at that staff dance, just know it,' Robin said.

Baby's face softened. 'Maybe something did, she smiled with a faraway look in her eyes 'Maybe I don't want to spend the summer being a ballerina. I want to be more . . . a part of things, that's all.'

'Part of what? The staff?' Robin looked at Baby as if she were crazy. 'It must be a guy, isn't it?'

'No. Yes. Robin, why does everything have to be about boys with you?'

Robin shook her head knowingly. 'Oh Baby, I'm thrilled. *Thrilled*. And don't worry, my lips are sealed. I won't tell a soul . . . ' She scurried off, elated, giving Baby a wave and a wink.

Baby shook her head and took a deep breath. She looked out of the window across the pool and stole a glance at Johnny, still seated with Sweets and Penny.

Sweets sipped a cup of coffee and looked curiously at Johnny.

'So, the old man likes the dance?' he asked Johnny.

'That's what he said.'

'*He* said that? Himself?' Sweets sounded surprised.

'Well, I guess he said it to Baby and she said it to us. Why?'

'Curious,' Sweets smiled. 'Just curious.' He emptied the cup of coffee and stood up. 'Time for my combo rehearsal. He smiled, as he walked away. So Max really liked it, huh?

Johnny frowned as Sweets left, confused by

the conversation. He looked after Sweets just as Max started making his morning rounds greeting guests in the pool dining area.

'So Mrs McCauly,' he overheard Max say at a guest's table, 'how's that adorable redhead of yours, Jeanie? We miss her this summer.'

Mrs McCauly smiled. 'She's marvelous. Traveling around Europe for the summer. And your girls?'

'Oh, they're fine. Baby's up here helping me out, as a matter of fact. I've made her talent co – co . . . '

Max trailed off and stared straight ahead in disbelief as he spotted Baby in her crisp waitress uniform taking an order from a young child. Max quickly excused himself from Mrs McCauly and started hastily after Baby, stopping to greet guests along the way, as she headed for the dining room.

Baby walked through the dining room into the kitchen. 'Tongue sandwich on rye, Gino,' she said to the chef.

'You see a tongue sandwich on the breakfast menu?' the chef asked.

'So the kid can't read – he still has to eat!' Baby laughed. 'Gimme a sandwich.'

'So make him a tongue sandwich yourself, I'm busy!' Gino snarled as he flipped over a row of pancakes on the griddle.

Baby moaned and grabbed a huge slab of tongue from the refrigerator. She placed it on the meat cutter just as Max appeared at her side.

'I sent you to the best schools, the best everything, for what? For you to be a waitress?' he shouted.

'Calm down, Dad. It's too early to be blowing your stack already.' Baby soothed. 'I decided to let someone who knows what he's doing take over again. That's all. Johnny is the talent co-ordinator as he should be. Besides,' she smiled at Gino across the slicer, 'I like this!'

'Since when do you do the hiring and firing?' her father asked. 'It's Johnny, isn't it? He's "wowed" you, hasn't he? I've seen him in action. He's "wowed" half the female population up here.'

Baby's face hardened. She put down the tongue and looked her father in the eye.

'Dad, I know I shouldn't say this, but you like "wowing" them yourself. This has nothing to do with Johnny and me.'

Max's face paled. 'Me? Wow 'em? What're you . . . ?'

'I might have been a kid back then, Dad, but I knew what was going on with you and your secretary . . . even if it didn't make sense till . . . '

'What secretary?' Max cried.

'It's OK, Dad.'

'What's OK?'

'You and Mom weren't getting along any-more. She wasn't young and attractive to you,' she said. 'You wanted to sow your wild oats.'

Max looked uncomfortable. 'What oats?' He took a deep breath, his eyes glaring. 'I should send you packing for talking to me like that!'

Baby smiled, still feeling the excitement of her dancing the night before. 'Look Dad, let's not fight. I'm happy to be here, happy to be a waitress making tongue sandwiches for break-fast. So why don't you just give me a hug?'

'You're too disrespectful to be hugged,' he said, turning away.

Baby took the tongue from the slicer and walked toward a stack of rye bread. She took two slices and put them on a plate,

'Dad, all I want is to have a job I can do well, make a few friends . . . get up there with the rest of them Saturday night . . . '

Max turned, his face fire engine red.

'Get up where?' Max boomed. 'You think I'm going to let you be in that – sideshow? I'll throw him and his cockamanie dance right out of . . . '

'No, Dad, don't,' Baby cried. 'You can't punish everyone 'cause of me!'

She sighed, her hands shaking as she sliced

the sandwich. 'All right, I won't be in it. I'm not good enough anyway. I'll stay away from Johnny and the dance. But let them do it. Don't spoil it for the others. It's a great dance. The guests will love it and the kids have worked so hard on it. Let them do it. I'll stay away.' Baby gulped.

'I have your word on that?' Max asked.

'You have my word,' she said after a moment. 'Do I have yours?'

Five

'I never minded that my dad worked in a fish store,' Norman said to the empty audience in the rehearsal hall. 'I always thought he should rent himself out at parties, you know, put him near a fan, turn it on, and you think you're having martinis on the Atlantic.'

Baby laughed out loud in the middle of the empty row of chairs.

'Come on,' Norman scowled, 'that's not funny.' He looked at her hopefully. 'Is it? Do you think it's funny?'

'No,' Baby smiled. 'I'm laughing so you'll get up there Saturday night and make a fool of yourself and make everyone miserable.'

Norman half-smiled, somewhat convinced. He crouched near the edge of the stage, beaming at Baby. Just then, Johnny walked in through the back door. He stopped in the shadows, unnoticed by Baby and Norman, and listened to their conversation.

'So, how come you're not getting up here Saturday night?' Norman asked.

Baby grimaced. 'I promised my father,' she said. 'He likes remembering me twirling around in my tutu. I gave him my word I'd stay out of it.'

She shrugged, a tear fighting its way back from the corner of her eye.

'It's OK. I didn't want to be in it anyway,' she said unconvincingly.

Norman sighed and stared adoringly at Baby. 'You know, if it hadn't been for you, I'd still be choking to death on dog jokes from the joke book.' He paused and took a deep breath. 'You really are . . . you really . . ' Norman trailed off, lost in her eyes, smitten by her smile of appreciation.

Baby grinned. 'C'mon, Norman, enough of this sentimental stuff. Aren't you supposed to be working tonight?'

'Gosh! You're right!' Norman said, jumping off the stage and grabbing his jacket. 'Look, Baby, if there's ever anything I can do for you . . . ' he hesitated and smiled. 'You know, simonize your living room, wallpaper your car, marry you . . . just let me know. Baby, I'm yours!' He blushed and ran out of the door as Baby smiled and laughed out aloud.

Johnny stood still in the shadows as Baby

looked around the deserted rehearsal hall. She heard the screen door slam shut as Norman bolted out and ran down the wooden steps. After a moment, she walked up onto the stage and stood there silently, her eyes closed, her head suddenly filling with the sounds of the dance music.

Slowly she started to move, gracefully doing a turn from the dance routine the group had rehearsed earlier. She swayed to the sounds in her head, silently moving, bending and reeling, feeling the power of the rhythm, a force outside herself.

Suddenly she stopped and looked around the empty room as the actual sounds of the music burst from the corner of the stage, She spun around bewildered as she spotted Johnny turning up the record player and emerging from the shadows.

Baby gasped.

'Hold that turn and you'll have it,' Johnny said, his voice full of praise.

'I . . . I was just . . . fooling around,' Baby stammered, unsettled that Johnny had seen her lost in the ecstacy of the dancing. 'I thought I could do it all . . . but after eight hours of waitressing, making tongue sandwiches for breakfast . . . '

Johnny walked out to the middle of the stage.

Baby felt her hands go cold in spite of the sweltering heat.

His piercing blue eyes stared straight into hers as he walked slowly and deliberately toward her.

'You looked OK to me,' he said softly, as the music played in the background.

Baby felt her knees shake, her heart quiver. 'I'll never be OK enough for Saturday night,' she said, trying to keep her normal voice.

Johnny took her hand. 'Tell you what,' he said, as he started to move to the rhythm of the music. 'You give it everything you got. If you *are* good enough, once you're up there your old man won't be able to do anything about it.'

'This doesn't have anything to do with my old . . . ' Baby stopped as she felt the warmth of his hand on her clammy palm.

'Look, you can't give up on what you had going just now. I saw you. You can move, you can do it. Don't give up. Not for him, not for me.' His gaze caused her heart to stop a beat.

'You?' Baby tried to look surprised.

'Don't kill yourself off inside all the time,' Johnny said, pulling her slowly into a dancing position. 'You gotta fight all the time.'

They stood close together as Johnny spoke. What if he hears my heart pounding, Baby thought, as she stared into his eyes.

'Keep believing in yourself,' Johnny said, as he began swaying with Baby. 'Every summer I come up here, my old man gets scared maybe I won't come home again . . . maybe I'll have the guts, know I can make it . . . and I'll be gone from his life, my other life. And he'll think he's lost me, 'cause I'm doing something he doesn't understand, but I can't let that stop me. You want to be in the dance, be in it!'

He pulled her closer as Baby responded and started to sway with him to the fiery, seductive music.

'That was good, real good,' Johnny said, as he wiped the sweat from his forehead. 'I told you. You can really move.'

Baby smiled. Her heart pounding. 'It felt good. I don't think I ever felt so good about anything,' she confessed. 'I felt so free!'

'That's the beauty of dancing,' Johnny smiled. 'It lets you be free, to be yourself, express yourself however you feel.'

'I love it. Thanks for the lesson,' Baby smiled.

'Listen,' Johnny said. 'We should practise again, maybe during your free time, when I don't have a lesson, so you can *really* feel confident.'

'Really? That would be great!' Baby said, figuring what her schedule would be.

'I have to set up for dinner now, but I have

some time before the cocktail hour at seven.'

'Great!' Johnny smiled. 'I'll meet you here about 5.30. OK?'

'Thanks, I'd love that. See you then,' Baby smiled. She flew off the stage and out of the rehearsal hall.

She raced through her table set-up and ran back for a quick shower before her next meeting with Johnny.

'I can't believe this,' Baby thought as she quickly shampooed her hair. 'Dancing with Johnny is so incredible! Just last week I was taking calculus finals and now I'm dancing . . . really dancing. What a riot!'

Robin sat on the bed of the cabin reading a movie magazine as Baby came dripping from the shower.

'Showering now? Isn't it early?' she asked, nonchalantly as Baby quickly dried herself, pulled her hair into a ponytail and jumped into a pair of shorts and a newly purchased halter top.

'Early? No, I'm kind of rushed today, Rob,' Baby said. 'Got to meet someone.'

'Who?' Robin asked curiously as Baby raced out the cabin, slamming the door before she could answer.

Johnny was waiting on the rehearsal hall stage, looking through a pile of 45s when Baby walked slowly in.

'Great!' he smiled. 'You made it. Let's get going.' He put a stack of records on the phonograph, jumped off the stage and pulled Baby into his arms.

'Ready?'

She nodded.

The music blasted and the pair danced in unison as the time flew by.

After an hour of practice, flushed and excited, Baby dashed back to her room and changed into a fresh uniform for the cocktail hour. She ran onto the dining-room patio where Sweets and the band were playing soft background music.

Baby grabbed a tray and began waiting on tables, fatigued and bleary-eyed but feeling a special energy inside. Sweets watched with amusement as she did a quick dance movement while balancing her tray.

'That's some kid,' he smiled to himself, as Baby tried to remember what Johnny had taught her. She stopped suddenly and stole a glance across the room where Max sat with Robin, talking and laughing, as they stared at Baby across the patio.

Max waved to Baby, summoning her to his table.

'Oh, waitress,' he said mockingly, 'could we have a bottle of champagne?' He smiled, 'Better still, why don't you just sit yourself down . . .

I'll get someone to cover your station . . . and I'll bring the champagne myself.'

Baby shook her head. 'No, Dad, not now. It's getting too busy out here.'

Max took her by the shoulders and pushed her into a chair.

'Sit down, young lady. We're going to celebrate,' he said, as he hurried off toward the bar.

Baby looked at Robin in bewilderment.

'I told him,' Robin finally said, bursting with glee. 'I had to. He was worried you weren't having any fun, so I told him how crazy you are about Neil and . . . '

'Neil?' Baby interrupted.

'Well, it wasn't hard to figure it out,' Robin said defensively. 'I know you said at first that he wasn't right for you but where else have you been every night?'

'With Johnny,' Baby said, scowling at her cousin.

'Not with Neil? Really?' Robin looked at her in amazement.

Baby shook her head and dropped it into her arms on the table.

'Boy, am I dumb,' she mumbled as Robin looked on confused.

'No, you're not,' Robin said, catching on. 'I tell everyone how bright you are.'

She paused and then did a double take.

'Johnny?'

'It's not what you think,' Baby said, half-lying, unsure herself if that were true. 'We've been rehearsing for the dance.'

Baby sighed deflatedly as she revealed her secret to Robin. 'My father's going to lock me in the canoe shed for the rest of the summer.'

Robin's mind raced, excited at the thought of an illicit romance.

'No, he won't, you're covered,' she said, energized by the challenge of the situation. 'As long as Uncle Max *thinks* you're dating Neil . . . what's the problem?'

'I'm *not* dating Neil!' Baby nearly shouted. She lowered her voice to a hoarse whisper. 'I hardly know Neil. Didn't I tell you that *you* should go after him?'

Robin shrugged. 'I'd love to. I even tried,' she admitted. 'But I'm not his type. Unfortunately. But you have to get to know him, now especially. He's gotta be better than the canoe shed.'

Baby looked at Robin, stymied by the situation, and groaned.

'OK,' she said. 'It looks like I have no choice. See you later.' Baby got up from the table and walked from the patio toward the pool. Moments later she stood next to Neil at the lifeguard chair.

'Hi!' she smiled cheerily.

'Hi!' he said, looking down at her from the elevated chair.

Baby took a deep breath. 'I was wondering if . . .'

'Go ahead,' Neil said smugly. 'Say it.'

Baby felt her face flush. 'This jerk isn't worth the effort,' she thought. 'But if my father finds out . . .'

'I really don't have anything to say except . . . except . . . ' she stammered uncomfortably.

Neil smiled confidently. 'You'd like to go out with me,' he said matter-of-factly.

Baby stared at him, stunned and embarrassed. 'No, not really. I mean, yes. How did you know?'

Neil sat tall in his lifeguard chair, very full of himself. 'Let's just say I know about these things. I would've asked you myself . . . I just didn't know if I wanted to get involved with anyone, going off to med school and all.'

Baby sighed with relief. 'Oh, we don't have to get involved or anything,' she said quickly.

Neil looked down, condescendingly. 'Come on, don't be shy! You're looking to grow up a little this summer, and you're thinking I might be the one to show you how it's done.'

Baby laughed to herself and tried to muster up some enthusiasm. She smiled brightly. 'I guess that must be it,' she said, exhaling slowly.

She turned suddenly as Max appeared with his bottle of champagne. He grinned up at Neil, high above it all in his seat of honor.

'You better take good care of my girl or I'll break that handsome nose of yours!' Max laughed.

'Yes, sir,' Neil said solemnly.

'Well, come on, let's celebrate!'

Neil hopped off the chair as Max put one arm around Baby and the other around Neil. Baby rolled her eyes to the heavens and sighed as Max led them from the pool to the patio to celebrate.

'Hey, Tony,' Neil called as he was led away, 'cover my chair for a while, will you?'

'Good thinking, my boy,' Max smiled, hugging Neil to him. 'Good thinking.'

Later that night, Baby was back in Johnny's arms, practising the dance. He lifted her in the air and she swerved, trying to catch herself.

'You're off tempo,' Johnny said angrily.

'I know.' Baby smiled sheepishly. 'I've been celebrating.'

He looked at her questioningly.

'My father thinks I'm dating Neil . . . so does Neil . . . so I had a glass of champagne,' she bubbled.

Johnny stared at her, his bright blue eyes darkening.

'It was that or telling my father the truth, which, believe me, it would have been a big relief to do . . . ' she rattled on. 'But then I'd have to spend the summer in the canoe shed and . . . '

She plopped into a nearby chair and started giggling.

Johnny looked at her angrily. 'I guess we're not going to get much work done now,' he said.

Baby flashed him a lopsided grin. 'Well,' she said, somewhat tipsily, 'we could just sit around, shoot the breeze, the wind, whatever.' She got up from the chair and walked over to Johnny, staring into his eyes. 'It's still early, isn't it?' she cooed.

'Not for you, young lady,' Johnny said, pointing toward the door.

'What do you think I am, twelve or something?' she asked testily. 'Don't you ever have any fun or anything?'

Johnny smiled. 'What kind of fun? You mean like holding you close . . . telling you what a thrill it is just to be near you?'

Baby's heart pounded as she stared at him, confounded, not knowing how to take it all in.

He shook his head and laughed. 'You curl up with your little diary . . . write something good. We'll pick this up tomorrow,' he said, as he looked at her with a bemused expression. Stil smiling, he walked away and out the door.

Baby stood alone in the rehearsal hall, her head starting to ache from the champagne, her heart throbbing from the scene with Johnny.

Disappointed and glum, she stared after him, then turned and walked out toward her room.

Baby awoke the next morning in a foul mood. Her head ached. Her mouth felt like paste.

'The last thing I need is to face those vultures at the breakfast table,' she growled as she banged off her alarm and jumped into the shower.

Half an hour later she stormed into the huge Kellerman's Hotel Kitchen and began rounding up her orders. She winced at the sound of the clanging frying pans, in spite of the two aspirins she'd taken.

Just then, Johnny walked up silently and touched her arm. She turned suddenly, dropping a plate of egg salad she was holding.

'Great! Just great!' she shouted, slamming down the tray as he bent to pick up the pieces. Johnny kneeled next to her, helping her with the broken plate.

'Feeling any better?' he asked, stifling a smile.

'Fine!' Baby growled at him. 'I love waking up feeling like a moron. It's one of my favorite . . . '

Johnny took her by the arm as she tossed the

egg salad remains into the garbage.

'Look, if we work tonight, we'll have it. I know you can do it!'

'I don't want to spend the night tramping through the woods practising that stupid turn,' Baby snapped.

'OK, then, we'll work at my place. In the staff area just over the bridge. See you around eight, OK?'

Before she could answer, a huge pair of feet stood before Baby and Johnny, who were again crouched on the floor as she sponged up the egg salad remains.

Baby and Johnny looked up as Neil stood above them.

'You all right, Baby?' Neil asked.

'Fine!' Baby gasped, freeing herself from Johnny's arm.

'I'll be waiting for you,' Johnny whispered to Baby, giving her a final look that made her heart leap into her throat. In an instant, he was gone.

'So,' Neil said, breaking into Baby's reverie, 'I was thinking we could have our first official date tonight.'

'Tonight?'

'It's Friday night, you can't spend it alone,' Neil laughed. 'I'll pick you up around eight, OK?'

'Around eight?'

'Come on,' Neil smiled. 'Don't be shy . . . give into it . . . '

Baby stared at him bleakly. 'Sounds great.'

Six

Neil stood in the doorway of Baby and Robin's room at eight as Robin bounced back and forth, like a tennis ball, blocking his view.

'You sure it's not just nerves?' Neil asked. 'Maybe if I just talk to her . . . '

'I told you, Neil,' Robin smiled. 'It was the bratwurst my parents sent up. She didn't have time to eat all day, she was working so much, and then she ate a whole brat. The poor kid's sick as a dog. You wanna take her out and have her throw up all over your new Chevy Impala?'

Neil shook his head, his face white with horror. 'No! Not the Impala! But I thought she wanted to go out with me.'

'She does. Just not tonight. Take a raincheck Neil and let Baby get better. She has to be up for the breakfast shift tomorrow and at this rate . . . she'll be sick all over the hotel. Uncle Max wouldn't like that!'

'I guess you're right,' Neil said, giving up easily as he walked away.

'Phew!' Robin sighed as she closed the door behind her and walked back into the empty room, slipping back onto the couch and polishing her toe nails.

At eight o'clock, Johnny put a record on his phonograph and heard a small knock at the door. He smiled and let Baby in. Without a word, he took her hand and started to lead her in the movements of the dance.

Baby held his gaze and danced with a new-found energy and spirit. She concentrated with delight as she mastered the complex series of turns and lifts.

The record played on and on. They danced wordlessly from song to song.

In the solace of her quiet cabin, Robin sat plucking her eyebrows when she suddenly heard a knock at the door.

'Uncle Max!' she cried in astonishment, as she opened the door.

'Neil told me Baby wasn't feeling well,' he said, as he stampeded into the room.

'Oh, well she's really fine, Uncle Max,' Robin babbled in rapid fire. 'It's just a . . . monthly thing. You know . . . a female monthly thing. Only, I couldn't very well say that to Neil, of course. But you understand, right, Uncle Max? She'll be fine in the morning, you'll see.'

She tried to guide him toward the door. 'Good night Uncle Max. I have everything under control here. Baby's fine with me.'

Max put his foot in the door as Robin tried to close it.

'Hold it, Robin, what's going on here?' he asked, pushing the door open and walking back into the room. 'Where is she?' he asked, after checking the room and the bathroom.

Robin sat on her bed. 'I can't tell you,' she said, holding her hand over her mouth.

'Where is she, Robin?' Max asked his voice rising in anger. 'I want a straight answer *now!*'

Robin's chin quivered. 'It's not fair!' she wailed. 'Why can't you let my lips stay sealed just once?'

Max stared at her and waited.

Robin stared back, trying to hold her resolve. Max stood silently, looking over her as she felt her resolve shrink and crumble.

'OK, Uncle Max, here's the story,' Robin sobbed as she reached for a box of tissues and started loudly blowing her nose.

In his room, Johnny stood at the record player, trying to decide which LP to put on, his back to Baby. He finally chose a disc, placed it on the turntable and music filled the air once more.

'Ready to try again?' Johnny asked, as he turned from the record player toward Baby.

When he turned, he found Baby sprawled on his bed, fast asleep. He walked over, and slowly smiled down at her. Just as he was reaching for a blanket to cover her, the screen door burst open.

Max stormed in like a tornado, Robin cowering behind him.

Johnny looked at Max and gently shook the sleeping girl.

'Baby, Baby wake up,' he called.

Robin started whimpering in the background. 'I had to tell him. Oh, my, this is all my fault. I'm going to kill myself, tie a rock around my neck and . . . '

Max turned. 'Shut up, Robin. That's enough out of you!'

Baby sat up, rubbed her eyes and saw the towering figure of her father, his face red with rage, standing above her.

Her heart sank as she looked at Johnny. Max grabbed her by the arm and pulled her out the door. As Max dragged Baby away from Johnny's room, Johnny and Robin stood silently watching them go.

Max walked quickly, silently. Baby glanced at him, walking double time to keep up with his fast pace.

'I should've asked you to believe me in the first place . . . When you see us on stage tomorrow night, it'll all make sense, I . . . '

'You think I'm going to keep him on here after *this*?' Max hissed.

'What do you think we were doing?' Baby asked, aghast.

'I know him, Baby.'

'What about me?' Baby cried. 'I'm the one you should know, but you don't. I can't go on all summer, feeling like I have to pass some kind of test with you. I've already gotten straight As, just to make you happy!'

Baby sprinted ahead of her father, then stopped suddenly and turned. 'You don't have to bother firing Johnny,' she shouted. 'Because I *quit*!'

'Wait a minute!' Max called. Baby stopped and stared at her father.

'Look in my eyes and tell me you believe I didn't do anything wrong,' she challenged.

She waited. Max looked at her, unable to suppress the doubt in his eyes.

'I knew it!' Baby shouted, turned and ran away.

'Baby!' Max called. 'Wait!'

She stopped and turned again. 'You deserve a peaceful summer, Dad . . . and I deserve more out of it than turning myself inside out to be your perfect Baby. I'm not a baby anymore . . . and I don't want to be perfect!!'

She turned and raced across the bridge back toward her room. Max started after her, then stopped himself and stood there, staring after her at a loss.

The next morning, Johnny went to Sweets' cabin, which was down the path from his. The early morning light spilled into the bare room as Sweets dressed himself in white pants and a flowered short-sleeve shirt. He stood in front of the mirror, brushing his afro as Johnny sat on the bed, fiddling with Sweets' saxophone.

'I don't get it,' Johnny said. 'The old man catches us like that . . . not that anything happened . . . I'm still here and she's leaving.' He sighed as Sweets took the sax from him and polished it lovingly.

'He knows if he wants her back he can't come down on you,' Sweets said. 'Nice, isn't it? She keeps saving your skin . . . and you keep thinking you deserve it!'

He eyed Johnny mockingly.

'I never asked her to do anything for me,' Johnny said, defensively.

'I'll bet you think she's even stupid for doing it, don't you?' Sweets said, his voice rising in anger.

'You know that girl has it ten times over you, Johnny. Just 'cause you fought your way out of the neighborhood, you think you're something special?'

'You don't think she had to put up a fight? You think being who she is came easy? And I'm not talking about being the boss's daughter. I'm talking about who she *is*. The kind of person she *is!*'

'Hey,' Johnny said, embarrassed by the put-down, 'if you're so freaked she's leaving, why're you driving her to the train station? Why don't you talk her out of it?'

Sweets shook his head and smiled, pointing to Johnny.

'All right, you're right. I'll talk her out of it,' Johnny said.

'Hey, man, don't bend yourself out of shape or anything,' Sweets said.

'I said I'd talk to her.'

Sweets laughed. 'I bet you think you can change her mind with that sexy smile of yours, don't you?'

Johnny beamed his best smile and made a thumbs-up signal.

'Wish me luck,' he laughed as he ran out the door.

* * *

Around noon, Johnny pulled his old red Chevy up in front of Baby and Robin's cabin and honked the horn.

Baby walked out, carrying her suitcases. As she looked up, she saw it was Johnny and stopped short.

'Where's Sweets?'

'He had a little car trouble,' Johnny said.

'Oh, well, I'll call a cab,' Baby said brusquely, as she turned back toward the cabin.

'Wait!' Johnny called. 'You got one, right here!'

He leaned over and opened the car door for her.

Baby hesitated.

'Come on,' Johnny coaxed. 'My conversation might not be good enough . . . but the car is.'

She stood a moment, thinking, then turned back toward the room.

'I'm going, Robin,' she called in through the screen.

Robin walked out to the porch, teary-eyed and miserable.

'All I wanted this summer was a little excitement,' she wailed. 'Not *Gone With the Wind*.'

Baby hugged Robin. 'You'll be fine,' she said warmly. 'And I'm glad we got to know each other again, even if it was for only a week. Good friends are hard to come by. But it doesn't take long to know when you have one!' Robin started to cry. Baby kissed her goodbye.

'Now, Robin, go wash your face, put on some of that new make-up and take a shot at Neil.' Baby smiled as she headed down the stairs. Robin nodded and waved, trying to muster a smile. She blew her nose loudly. Baby grabbed her suitcases, threw them in the back seat and got into Johnny's car.

Johnny headed out down the long winding road from Kellerman's. Baby took one last look back and sighed. Had it really been one week? In such a short time she'd lived a whole different chapter in her life. So much had happened she could hardly believe it. Johnny. The dance. Her father. Robin. Neil. Norman. Even waitressing. Roslyn seemed a million miles away after this time capsule of a life in the mountains.

Music played from the radio as they drove along the country road leading to the Monticello train station, the same station she'd come from the week before with the chatty cab driver. Both Baby and Johnny were silent now. After a few moments, Johnny stopped the car, turned up the radio and got out.

He motioned to her seductively with his hand. 'Come on, you never did get that turn right,' he said, moving to the beat of the music. Baby stared at him in silence from the passenger seat of the car.

'OK,' Johnny said, as he walked to the car and reached out for her. 'Forget the turn. Just dance with me. You gotta let me have one last dance.'

'Why?'

Johnny swept her into his arms. He pulled her close, taking her breath away as he led in a slow, but highly charged, sensual dance, their bodies moving in unison. Baby followed his lead, surprised and touched by what she saw in his twinkling blue eyes. Finally, he drew her even closer and kissed her, slowly and sweetly. Baby yielded to the kiss, her eyes closed, her heart fluttering.

He eased her back gently, took her by the hand and led her to the car. Johnny opened the door and Baby got into the front seat. He went around to the other side, started the car and turned it around, heading back to Kellerman's.

'Wait!' Baby said. 'The train station is the other way.'

'I know.'

'No,' Baby said, 'things are going too fast. Turn the car around.'

'You'll catch up,' Johnny smiled seductively. 'Look, your old man thinks the worst of both of us right now . . . You get up there tonight, he'll

have to eat it whole. I can't wait to see his face
when you . . . '

'No!' Baby shrieked, shaken and angry. 'Stop
the car!'

Johnny slowed the car, surprised by the tone
in her voice. Baby opened the door while the car
was still moving and got out. Johnny slammed
on the brakes and stared at her as she hauled her
suitcases out of the back seat and started walking toward the train station. He quickly backed
up the car alongside her.

'What're you doing? It's twelve miles to the
train station!' he called out the window.

Baby turned and put down her suitcases,
gasping for breath. 'You think one kiss from you
changes everything?' she shouted furiously.
'You think that's all I needed?'

Johnny shook his head. 'Call it my best shot,'
he said gently. 'A little added incentive. Look
. . . I *do* like you.'

'I don't want you liking me!' Baby shouted. 'I
– want – a . . . ' She took a deep breath, pulling
herself together. 'All I ever wanted from you
was to learn how to dance!'

'Then get up there and dance!' Johnny shouted
as Baby picked up her suitcases and continued
walking down the long dusty road to the train.

Johnny leaned on his horn, trying together to
stop and look at him. Finally, angrily, he gave

up, spun the car around and speeded off back in the direction of Kellerman's.

Baby stopped and looked back over her shoulder at the disappearing car. She sat on her suitcases and cried.

Later that night it was showtime at Kellerman's and Norman was center stage, finishing the routine about his father and the fish store, soaking up the audience's obviously appreciative laughter. The dancers waited in the wings, preparing for their number following Norman's comedy routine. Baby slipped in behind them, unnoticed.

The audience roared as Norman finished his routine. He beamed at the standing ovation and took a bow.

'Thank you, thank you,' he oozed, 'and I'd really like to thank one particular person who isn't here tonight . . . a girl I hope will be my "Annette" in my next incarnation as Frankie Avalon.'

Baby came in through the back door unnoticed as Norman gave her his tribute. She smiled and stood silently against the social hall wall.

After three hours at the train station, nursing her aching feet, she had decided to come back to the hotel and literally face the music, including that of her father and Johnny. So here she stood,

as Sweets and the musicians readied themselves
for the big musical number.

The kids in the dance number were checking
their make-up, stockings and practising those
few tricky steps in the final moments before
curtain time. Baby stood silently, watching the
drama and excitement behind the stage, which
seemed almost more exciting than what was
happening on the stage itself.

This was to be her big test, she knew. The first
time she would not only dance like she'd never
danced before, or even dreamt she could. It was
also the first time she had ever really defied her
father. The thought of both challenges fright-
ened and exhilarated her. Baby took special
pride in hearing the warm reception Norman,
her comedy protégé, was receiving. The audience laughed and applauded, and Baby smiled
to herself. Norman bowed again and handed the
microphone to Max.

'Thanks Norman,' Max said. 'Great job. That
boy's on the way to being the next Jack Benny,
right, folks! And you saw it first right here at
Kellerman's!' The audience hooted and howled
as Max led another round of applause for a red-
faced Norman who ran out for a final bow.

Max cleared his throat. 'And now we have a
dance for your enjoyment which someone told
me you would like . . . so that's why we're

doing it. Hope she's right.'

The lights had dimmed and the curtain was closed as Max moved from the stage. Behind the curtain, the dancers took their position, with Johnny center stage.

As the music blared, the curtain parted and Johnny and the dancers broke into their hot and sexy dance routine, captivating the audience, most of whom loved it and clapped and swayed along. Max scanned the room to gauge the reaction.

'Most of them seem to like it,' he admitted, although he spotted a few of the older guests with disapproving grimaces on their faces.

Max looked back on stage just as Baby joined the group at the rear. She jumped into the motion without missing a beat, dancing with an intensity she had not shown before, a determination to succeed and shine.

As the number reached the moment of the impossibly difficult series of consecutive turns, Baby performed brilliantly, her face radiant, her body in perfect synchronization. Johnny stared at her even as she danced, amazed and enthralled.

Max watched from the wings, both proud and appalled at the same time as he saw that his Baby had, in fact, really grown into a young woman.

Norman stood at his side, enchanted by the vision of Baby.

'She's great, Max, isn't she great!' Norman repeated.

Max shook his head silently, disconcerted and somewhat unable to comprehend this new, fiery Baby.

'We wanted her to be a ballerina,' he said to no one in particular as he shook his head.

Cheers and a standing ovation delighted the sweaty and exhausted staff dancers who basked in the glory of the applause. They hugged each other behind the curtain, congratulating themselves on a startling new moment at traditional old Kellerman's hotel.

'You were great! How did you learn that so fast?' Several dancers bombarded Baby with compliments.

'Thanks,' she smiled, slipping away from the crowds as she spotted her father, standing somewhat shell-shocked in the wings.

'So what did you think?' she asked him.

'I think they loved it,' he admitted. 'I also think you worked very hard . . . I should've known that all along. If I'm lucky, maybe I'll learn a few things this summer.'

'So you want to keep me on?' Baby asked.

Max gulped. 'If you give me the chance.'

'How else am I going to prove to you what a

fine, nearly perfect daughter you raised?' she laughed.

'Hey, Baby,' Norman called, 'you coming to the party?'

Baby turned and stared at Norman and the kids and then turned back to her father.

'Why don't you go celebrate with your friends?' Max said, nudging her toward the staff.

Baby looked at him and Max smiled, as encouragingly as he could. She threw her arms around her father, kissed him with a peck on the cheek and ran off with the staff.

The staff dance room was hot and sweaty, music blared, couples moved slowly and slinkily. A relaxed, laid-back atmosphere filled the smoky room. Suddenly, the music changed and the dancers celebrated their success in a frenzy, with bodies gyrating, sexy and suggestive twists and turns and wild whoops of laughter filling the room. In one corner, Johnny danced with Baby, more slowly and seductively than the others, as he took her in with his eyes, caressing her with a new gentleness, never moving his gaze from hers.

'You were really something tonight,' Johnny whispered in her ear. Baby's spine tingled with excitement. 'I didn't think you had it in you, but you certainly do.'

She smiled.

'Life is full of small surprises,' she said, gazing back into his sexy blue eyes.

'So maybe there's a future for us, after all?' Johnny asked.

'I told you,' Baby said, trying to control her own excited hormones, 'all I wanted was to learn how to dance.'

He looked up at her, hurt and surprised.

Baby grinned, turned and, before he could stop her, was gone, lost in the crowd of frenzied and excited dancers.

In the bar, Sweets jingled a soulful tune on the piano. Max walked up with a beer.

'Where's Baby?' Sweets asked Max who stared mournfully into the mug of beer.

'Probably off ruining her life,' Max said. 'Nothing I can do about it . . . just care less . . . have a few more beers. Right, Sweets?'

Sweets shook his head.

'Don't you go worrying about that Baby of yours, Max. She's a real lady. She'll always make you proud.'

Johnny stood outside the staff dance room, leaning against the railing, staring down at the wooden plank porch, feeling empty and pensive.

Penny tiptoed out and stood quietly next to him.

'What happened to the boss's daughter?' she asked, trying to hide her jealousy and pleasure.

'Probably foxtrotting with Daddy,' Johnny shot back cynically. 'Who cares? She's not part of this and who wants her to be?'

He leaned against the railing, swaying to the music, his eyes closed, recalling his dance with Baby.

At that moment, Baby was swaying to the same tune, indelibly inscribed on her mind, dancing in the woods, alone, under a near-perfect, brilliant moon, feeling sultry, satisfied and very much at peace with the world.

Seven

Sunday morning dawned bright and sunny at Kellerman's. It was back to work for the exhilarated staff members who were still on a high from their Saturday night dancing success.

The hot July sun baked across the green lawns and soon after breakfast the pool was already packed with guests seeking relief.

A mock-up New York City subway was the center of attention at the pool as a crowd of people gathered around, among them five photographers.

'I'm so glad you're back, Baby,' Robin said. 'I don't think I could have lasted the summer without you!'

'Me too.' Baby admitted. 'Although, I guess you could say I never *really* left.' The cousins stood under a brilliant mountain sun, dripping wet from a dip in the cool, pool water. Both girls were wearing modest bathing suits, as they

watched the excitement surrounding the subway scene. Norman stood with them as the
subway door dramatically opened and an exquisite twenty-six year old brunette sporting a
sexy and very revealing bathing suit emerged. A
banner, draped over her suit, read *Miss Subways*.
She waved and beamed a radiant smile to the
cheering onlookers, including a smitten, red-
faced Max Kellerman.

'On behalf of Kellerman's,' Max boomed into a
microphone, 'I'd like to welcome Giselle Peridot
. . . straight from New York City, via Belgium
. . . "Miss Subways" . . . July 1963!'

Neil stood jauntily at the side of the crowd,
eyeing the svelte Miss Subways.

'Now *that's* a woman,' he said to himself, as
he flexed his biceps, pulled in his stomach and
walked over to the radiant beauty to have a
photo taken with her.

'Miss Peridot,' Neil smiled. 'I'm Neil Mumford, the lifeguard here at Kellerman's.'

'How do you do?' she smiled as the crowds
pushed forward.

'If you'd like to put that swimsuit to work, I'd
be happy to give you a lesson,' he said gallantly,
beaming a big Pepsodent smile.

'Oh, thank you, but I do not swim,' she
laughed. 'The swimsuit is only for, how you say,
the people?'

Neil blushed and was pushed back into the crowd.

The photographers gathered around, snapping madly as Giselle stood in various seductive poses, putting her arms around blushing old men and shaking hands with gawking teenagers.

'Gee, I love mass transit,' Norman sighed, as he ogled the beauty queen.

'Ugh!' Robin groaned. She sucked in her stomach. 'I'm never going to ride the subway again!'

Baby looked down at her own suit and straightened her back. 'I'm never going to wear a bathing suit again,' she moaned as she eyeballed Giselle's long slim legs, exquisite skin and hourglass figure.

As she looked toward the subway scene, Baby gasped as she saw the beauty queen kissing her father passionately on the cheek for a photographer.

'Do you believe your father?' Robin said, nudging Baby as she caught the same scene. 'He is totally gaga!'

'He's not gaga,' Baby snapped, trying to cover her concern. 'It's just a publicity thing. That's why she's here.'

Behind the girls, two old ladies staying at the hotel were watching the same spectacle.

'His wife would be turning over in her grave,' one said. 'That is, if she was dead!'

'*Men, feh,*' her companion agreed. 'The older they get, the more foolish they become.'

Baby blushed as she overheard the conversation and focused on her smiling, blushing father.

'Oh my,' she thought. 'He *is* gaga!'

'I've got to go,' Baby said suddenly to Robin and Norman. 'Time to get ready for the lunch crowd.'

'All these people do is eat!' Norman laughed.

'That's what you come to the country for!' Robin said defensively. 'It's probably the best part!'

Baby laughed.

'I'll come with you,' Robin said.

'So,' Robin asked Baby, as she headed back to the cabin with her, 'what's on the menu today? I'm starved!'

They passed the rehearsal hall on the way to their cabin. Baby and Robin heard the strains of hot rhumba music. 'Boy, I wish I could move like that Penny,' Robin sighed. 'She really knows how to put it all in the right places. And what a figure! So tell, me, Babes, what's for lunch?'

Inside, Johnny and Penny rehearsed a steamy version of the dance, their moves slinky and suggestive.

The pair moved as one, their years of dancing together evident by the casual confidence each expected from the other. They slid, skidded and wiggled around the floor as Johnny executed a spectacular final move. The sound of applause echoed in the empty hall as the music suddenly stopped. Johnny turned to see Max, clapping his hands, watching from the doorway.

Johnny looked back at Penny, his eyebrows raised with surprise and concern, fearful that the number would be considered too sexy by Max.

'Hi, Mr Kellerman,' Johnny said, as he jumped effortlessly off the stage and walked over to his boss.

'Johnny, that number . . . ' Max began.

'Oh, it'll be a lot different by the Miss Subways dance tomorrow night,' Johnny said quickly interrupting Kellerman.

'I like it,' Max said.

Johnny looked stunned.

'You do?'

'I have a favor to ask you, Johnny,' Max said, as Penny walked discreetly out the back door.

'Uh, sure. What?'

'First, I need your word. This is our secret, OK?'

Johnny raised his eyebrows again but nodded in agreement. 'Anything you say, Mr Kellerman. My lips are sealed.'

Max pulled Johnny over to a seat and whispered furtively.

'OK, Mr Kellerman,' Johnny said. 'No problem. We'll meet you back here around four.'

'Great, and thanks, Johnny,' Max said, as he walked jauntily out of the rehearsal hall whistling.

Penny walked back through the rear door when she heard Max leave.

'What's that all about?' she asked.

Johnny smiled.

'You won't believe this,' he chuckled. 'Just be here at four. See you then.'

At 3.45, Max Kellerman walked nonchalantly toward the rehearsal hall, looking around to see if he was noticed. He waved to several guests walking in the late afternoon coolness, then ducked unseen into the hall.

Moments later, the sound of cha-cha music boomed through the rehearsal hall as Max stood holding Penny in his arms.

Johnny leaned near the record player, counting out the rhythm, as Penny stood in high heels in a dancing position with Max. Her face showed both amazement and terror as she tried to teach her boss to dance. She stifled a laugh as she pictured the scene.

'OK,' Johnny called, 'on the four.'

'On the four,' Max repeated, uncomfortably

holding his arms around Penny who was wearing a skimpy halter top. 'Got it.'

'And remember, the important thing is to relax. This is fun!'

Standing ramrod straight, Max stiffened even more. 'I am relaxed,' he said, his face tense and serious.

'OK – *four* five, six . . . *four*, five six.'

Max tried to follow Penny and the rhythm, counting outloud along with Johnny. '*Four*, five, six . . . *four*, five six.'

Within a few minutes Max was indeed dancing a very rough imitation of the cha-cha.

'I can't go from four . . . ' he complained as he missed the beat. 'It's like starting the alphabet from G!'

Losing his concentration, he stepped hard on Penny's toe. She winced as her foot began to throb.

'Sorry,' Max said.

'That's OK,' Penny smiled. 'No problem.'

The record droned on as Max and Penny continued to repeat the *four*, five, six pattern with minimal success.

Max counted out loud. '*Four*, five, six. *Four*, five, six . . . ' He stepped hard once again on Penny's toe. '*Four*, five—'

Penny's face contorted with pain and she hopped on one foot.

'Oh, God . . . ' she whispered.

'Are you OK?' Johnny asked.

'Fine,' Penny tried to smile. 'I'm going to be fine. I just need a minute. Excuse me, Mr Keller-man,' she said, as she hobbled off to one side.

Penny limped back to the kitchen for some ice as Johnny put the cha-cha record on one more time.

'OK, Mr Kellerman, let's go for it,' Johnny said, as Max continued to count 'Four, five, six. Four, five, six . . . '

Penny returned and sat on the side, her foot throbbing with pain, as she held an ice pack to it. She bit her lip to keep from laughing out loud as she watched the scene before her.

Standing on stage in the rehearsal hall, Max Kellerman was trying to lead Johnny Castle in the cha-cha!

'I wish I had a camera for this one,' Penny laughed to herself.

'Did anyone ever tell you you have beautiful eyes,' Max said to Johnny as he tried to do the dance.

'Will you just dance?' Johnny shot back, losing patience with his clumsy two-left-footed boss.

'Four, five, six,' Max chanted.

Suddenly Max landed hard on Johnny's foot. 'Sorry.'

Johnny winced, trying to hide the pain. 'These things happen.'

Johnny took a deep breath and stopped dancing. 'Look, Mr Kellerman, I got an idea. You know the fox trot. Why don't you stick to that?'

'Giselle is not a fox trot, Johnny,' Max said angrily. 'I'm escorting her to the big "do" tomorrow night, in her honor. I've got to be . . . oh, *you* know!'

Johnny smiled. 'Mr Kellerman, I'm only a dance instructor. I'm not a brain surgeon. I think you've got a mental block here . . .'

Suddenly Max's face turned red. He grabbed Johnny by the shirt. 'Johnny,' he rasped. 'I've *got* to cha-cha!'

'Right,' Johnny said, putting Max's arms around him again. 'Let's go . . . And – *four*, five, six. *Four*, five six . . .'

Eight

The patio dining room was illuminated with pink and white candles on each table. Tiny flecks of lights entwined the surrounding trees.

Sweets played a romantic tune on the piano, and a star-filled sky and a full moon completed the picture of a perfect night.

Max sat across from Giselle under the starry sky, wearing an impeccable white dinner jacket. She fluttered her long lashes at the greying hotel owner and pulled back her shoulders, emphasizing the sexy figure inside her form-fitting pink strapless gown.

' . . . I was far-sighted,' Max said, as he gazed into her blue-green eyes, realizing he couldn't concentrate on conversation because his gaze kept sliding down to her dress.

Giselle smiled attentively, taking in every word, flashing a "come hither look" with her eyes.

'I had a weak stomach and I couldn't stand

heights,' Max rambled. 'So, of course, they put me in the Air Corps.'

Giselle's eyes sparkled.

'Ah? You were a flier?'

'No,' Max laughed. 'Somebody wised up. I won the war behind a desk in Sioux Falls, South Dakota.'

Giselle's smile faded and she looked suddenly remote. 'My father . . . he was . . . ' She looked down as a tear trickled across her cheek. 'He was a very brave man.'

'A pilot?' Max asked.

'No. He fought with the Resistance. He died for our country,' she said, wiping her eyes with a pink linen napkin.

'I'm sorry,' Max whispered, as he reached out and squeezed her hand.

'My mother says I do not stop looking for him,' Giselle laughed. 'For a while I had, how do you say, a serious boyfriend. He was . . . older. Like my father. With a man like that I feel more . . . what . . . '

'Comfortable?' Max finished the sentence.

'Comfortable. Yes. A good word. Comfortable. Like I feel now,' Giselle smiled and squeezed Max's hand.

They gazed at each other silently for a long time, holding hands.

'I don't say this often . . . I don't say it at

all . . . ,' Max stammered. 'What I want to say is . . . '

'I know, I feel the same way, Max,' Giselle cooed, as she leaned forward seductively.

Max smiled, his eyes moist, his heart and groin pounding. A waiter approached the table.

'Can I get you anything, Mr Kellerman?' he asked.

'Champagne,' Max said without losing eye contact with Giselle. 'The most expensive bottle we have.'

'Yes, sir. Right away,' the waiter said.

'And would you send it to my room?' Max asked.

'Yes,' Giselle smiled. 'That would be nice.'

'To your room, sir?' the waiter asked in amazement.

'Yes,' Max sighed blissfully, as he rose and took Giselle by the hand. 'To my room.'

Sweets' fingers twinkled across the keyboard as he watched Max lead Giselle from the dining room, arm in arm.

'That man never gonna learn,' he sighed, shaking his head. 'He's looking for trouble.'

The next morning, Giselle and Max were out on the shuffle board court together under the suspicious, watchful eyes of the two old ladies who were guests at the hotel.

'The trick is to follow through smoothly,' Max explained, demonstrating as he shoved a disc toward a triangle. The disc slid on the board and continued past it.

Max laughed. 'Of course, it helps if you land on one of the numbers. That's the object.'

'A strong man like you,' Giselle cooed, fluttering her bedroom eyes,' you can't help yourself pushing it so hard.'

'Right,' Max smiled, loving every minute of this. 'I can't help it. I was born this way. Musculature.' He handed her the stick. 'Now you try.'

Giselle took the stick and tried to imitate how to place it next to the disk.

'Wait, I'll show you,' Max smiled, as he wrapped his arms around her slim waist to demonstrate the proper method.

He helped her shove the disk down the board where it actually managed to land in a triangle. Giselle jumped up and down jiggling excitedly, hugging and squeezing Max with passionate enthusiasm. Max hugged her back just as Baby, dressed in tennis whites and carrying her racket, was heading toward the courts below.

Baby stopped suddenly as she spotted the embrace and stared at her father. Engrossed in Giselle, Max didn't notice Baby. He released Giselle from his bear hug and reached into his pocket, handing her a beautiful leather jewelry case.

'For you,' Max beamed, as Baby watched unnoticed from the sidelines. 'To make you even more beautiful, if possible.'

Giselle shook her head, smiling coyly. 'No, no, Max . . . I could not.'

'But you must,' Max insisted, as he opened the box and lifted out a gorgeous strand of pearls.

'Oh Max, pearls!' Giselle beamed. 'Oh, thank you, Max. Thank you so much!'

Max smiled and fastened the pearls around her neck.

The two old ladies had stood in place watching the entire exchange between Max and Giselle. They huddled in a corner, chattering madly, as Baby stood behind them listening.

'Pearls, not bad,' the bleach-blonde lady said, with a strong Brooklyn accent.

'Eh, pearls,' her friend shrugged. 'They're not diamonds!'

'Diamonds?' the blonde laughed. 'Who gets diamonds these days? Even if you look like her!'

The ladies shook their heads. 'The man is out of control. Giving her presents like that! Why, he hardly knows her. It's embarrassing! What a fool!'

'Don't worry,' the blonde shook her head, winking. 'He knows her. He knows!'

Suddenly Max looked up from Giselle and saw Baby standing near the old ladies. She glared at him, spun on her heels and stalked away.

That night, guests dressed in gowns and jewels headed to the grand ballroom for the special evening in honor of Miss Subways. Baby was off duty that night and she was dressed in a smart royal blue cocktail dress, her hair pinned up in an attractive French knot. She was walking up the stairs to the ballroom when she noticed Max, with Giselle on his arm.

'Hey, Honey,' Max called.

Baby ignored him and kept walking. Max whispered something to Giselle who headed up the stairs toward the head table in the ballroom. Max followed Baby.

'All right,' Max said, taking Baby by the arm. 'What's wrong?'

Baby turned and stared at her father. 'You hardly know her and you're giving her pearls!'

Max shuffled defensively. 'They're just cultured pearls,' he said.

'They're expensive! And you gave them to her at . . . at shuffle board! In front of all those *yentas* who are gossiping their heads off about what an old fool you are.' She looked down. 'It's just so . . . so sad to me.'

'Sad?' Max looked incredulous. 'Sad? I'm having the best time I've had in . . . '

'I know that,' Baby interrupted.

'So what are you saying?' Max asked. 'I'm not allowed to enjoy myself, have a little fun, some happiness?'

Baby sighed. 'I knew when you and Mom split up you'd wind up with someone one day . . . but *her*? She's just like that sleazy secretary . . . '

'I haven't wound up with anyone,' Max argued. 'And what's wrong with her?'

'What was wrong with *Mom*?' Baby shouted. 'When did you stop loving her? When she wasn't young and beautiful anymore?'

Max's face turned beet-red. 'That doesn't deserve an answer,' he said, outraged.

'Fine. Then we have nothing to talk about!' Baby turned and stalked away as Max stood looking after her, shaking inside and feeling more than a little uncomfortable.

As Baby wove her way into the crowds, Max turned and walked to his table in the ballroom where Giselle sat waiting, fingering the beautiful pearls.

A big streamer hung on the stage curtain, reading *Welcome Miss Subways*. Below the streamer, Sweets and his combo performed for the dancers who moved happily and gracefully around the wooden dance floor.

Max walked over to Giselle. 'May I have this dance?' he smiled, bowing grandly.

'But of course!' she cooed, as she wiggled in a tight white satin gown over to the dance floor and slid into Max's waiting arms. Max danced with Giselle, trying hard to make the best of his dancing lessons. He kept hearing Johnny's count in his head 'Four, five, six, four, five, six' and forced himself to relax.

After a few minutes of looking at Giselle and remembering the evening he had spent with her the day before, he relaxed with ease and really began to enjoy himself. Baby watched angrily from the sidelines.

The music stopped and the dancers applauded, moving from the center of the floor where Johnny and Penny began an exhibition dance with a flourish.

The instructors were captivating and the guests stood around, watching their magical movements. Johnny wore tight black tails which showed off his muscular body. Penny's flashy red chiffon played up her tiny waist and gorgeous legs as they wiggled, twisted and turned in synchronization. Max and Giselle backed off to the sidelines as the guests crowded around in delight to watch the floor show.

Several guests got between Max and Giselle, separating them as they watched Johnny and Penny execute the flashy rumba with pizzaz and precision.

The guests sighed, cheered and applauded.

Giselle clapped enthusiastically with the rest of the guests, her eyes fixated on Johnny's sexy body and svelte moves.

Johnny and Penny finished their exhibition with a flourish and broke away from each other, moving into the crowd. Penny headed for a male guest and asked him to dance, to his obvious delight.

Max looked up and paled as he saw Giselle emerge from the sidelines and walk straight out toward Johnny, offering herself as a partner.

Sweets watched from the stage as he led the band, feeling sorry for his old friend Max whose disappointment and embarrassment were more than obvious.

Johnny smiled and led Giselle in elaborate turns, ending with the pair pressing closely against each other. Giselle's eye glistened and sparks flew as she stared into Johnny's blue eyes. Johnny winked and bowed in appreciation as Max approached the couple.

'Giselle, will you excuse us?' Max said as he pointed toward his table. 'Johnny and I need to discuss business for a moment.'

He almost pushed Johnny off the dance floor and out of the ballroom.

In the hallway, Max grabbed Johnny's arm, his face red and sweaty.

'Could you just this once keep your hands off?' he hissed as Johnny looked up in surprise.

'I was dancing with the guests like always . . .' Johnny started to explain.

'This is *my* guest,' Max said, regaining his composure and letting go of Johnny's arm. 'Promise me you'll steer clear . . . do me a favor.'

'Sure,' Johnny said, brushing his jacket smooth. 'No problem.'

Max headed back to Giselle. Johnny stood in the hallway for a moment and watched him, shaking his head. Baby walked up next to Johnny as they looked into the ballroom where Max was once again dancing with Giselle. Sweets was watching from the bandstand shaking his head.

'What'd he say?' Baby asked.

'Nothing important.'

'I'm worried about him,' she confided.

'He's a big boy,' Johnny smiled. 'He'll be fine.'

Nine

The full moon cast a bright shadow across the bed in Johnny's cabin that night where he lay sprawled, sound asleep. His arms were outstretched across the crisp white pillows, his legs, bent roundly under the covers. Suddenly the shadow broadened as a crack of light came through the door, which opened silently while Johnny slept.

Giselle stood silhouetted in the moonlight and closed the door behind her. She walked up to Johnny's bed, clutching an expensive but very sheer robe around her slim body, looked down at his handsome face, and smiled.

She dropped the robe to the floor, slipped into Johnny's bed and gently pressed up against him. Johnny stirred, pulling the sheets up against his neck, but he didn't awaken. Giselle moved closer, kissed his neck, then his ears. Johnny's eyes opened suddenly. He turned toward her, astonished.

She smiled and pulled him to her in a deep kiss.

Johnny was fully awake by now. He eased Giselle away from him.

'What are you doing here?' he asked softly.

'I wanted to see you again.' she whispered, rubbing his chest.

'This is very different than *seeing me*.' Johnny said, smiling. 'I'd call it . . . '

She leaned in and kissed him hard, silencing him before he could finish speaking. She felt soft and warm and at first he didn't resist.

'Wait . . . wait . . .' Johnny said, pushing her away, 'this is . . . '

'Shhh, don't talk, 'Giselle whispered, nibbling on his ear. '*We* don't need words between us.' She kissed him again. Johnny finally eased back. Giselle kissed him again. Johnny shook his head suddenly and fiercely and got out of his bed.

'Giselle,' he said, pulling on a bathrobe, 'you gotta go . . . '

She looked at him, confused. Johnny picked up her robe and tossed it to her.

'You don't find me attractive?' she asked.

'That's not the point.'

'Then what is?'

'Aren't you forgetting about somebody?'

Giselle laughed. 'Max? You Americans! On

some things you are so . . . so simple! In my
country . . . in Europe, things are different. We
know how to have fun.'

Johnny took a deep breath. 'Let's just say I'm
not feeling very European tonight.'

Giselle grabbed her robe, angry and insulted.
'Have it your way. You will be sorry!'

She glared at him, tied her robe around her
tiny waist and ran out of the cabin, slamming
the door.

Johnny sat on the bed and shook his head.

'Women,' he said as he crawled back under
the sheets and tried to get back to sleep.

The next morning, Max sat anxiously at the patio
breakfast table. Baby watched him as he looked
all around, while she served a table nearby.

Suddenly, she noticed his mood change as
Giselle approached from across the room. Baby
sighed and walked toward the coffee pot at her
waitress stand.

'Well, good morning,' Max said as he pulled
out a chair for Giselle. 'I was worried about you.'

'Worried?' Giselle looked innocently confused.

'I, uh, stopped by your room last night. You
said you wanted to go to bed early, but you
weren't there.'

'Oh, Max,' Giselle said hesitantly, 'I don't

know how to tell you this.'

'What?'

'Your dance teacher . . . ' Giselle said, shaking her head.

'Johnny? What about him? What did he do?' Max demanded.

Giselle looked down at her lap and patted her eyes with the napkin. 'He is a . . . very rude man.'

Max's face reddened. 'In what way?'

'Well,' she began, 'he followed me after the party. He stopped me . . . and . . . '

By now Max sat white-knuckled, his blood pressure rising as Giselle played the ingenue.

'What?'

'He wanted me,' she started. 'He told me . . . he want to . . . make love with me!'

Max stared at her in shock. Baby stopped in her tracks, nearly burning herself on the hot pot of coffee, as she overheard the exchange.

'Why didn't you come to me?' Max demanded.

'I was . . . confused. I thought if I told you . . . you would be so angry . . . it would cost him his job.'

Giselle stared at him sadly and demurely, fluttering her long lashes, as Max's rage boiled He pushed back his chair, jumped up and stormed off the patio as Giselle made hersel comfortable at the breakfast table and began reading the day's menu. Baby stared back at Giselle, appalled and angry.

Max ran across the moist morning lawn, stormed into the ballroom rehearsal hall where Johnny was standing by the record player with three or four of the dancers.

'Let's try the number to *She's A Fool*,' he said. 'Maybe that'll work.'

Before he could put the record on the machine, Max was at his side, glaring at Johnny.

'OK, I want you *out* of here, *now*, Mr Castle,' he bellowed. 'Pack your records and your long hair and your tight blue jeans and get out of my sight!!!'

Johnny stood gaping as the kids began whispering around him. Max did an about-face and stalked out of the door without giving Johnny a chance to speak.

Johnny threw down the record and ran out the door of the rehearsal room, stopping in his tracks as he nearly ran into Baby who was running toward him.

'Hey, Bab—' he started, cut off suddenly as she slapped him across the face.

Johnny jumped back and stared at her, stunned.

'What the . . . ?'

'You just had to do it, did you?' she shouted, livid with rage.

'Do what?'

'Some pretty girl comes up here . . . *any* pretty girl . . . and she's immediately your territory, right? It doesn't matter who else might be interested in her!'

'Hold on a minute, there,' Johnny shouted angrily.

'But, hey, what do you care?' Baby interrupted. 'You just got another notch in your headboard!'

'What the hell're you talking about?' Johnny asked.

'What do you *think* I'm talking about?' she yelled.

'I have no idea!' he said, looking truly confused.

'Well, your little Belgium waffle sure had a good idea!' Baby sputtered as she turned on her heels and ran away. Johnny stood, watching her go, as he tried to absorb what she said.

'Why that . . . ' Johnny said angrily. He bolted toward the main house and walked up to Giselle's room.

Giselle was sitting in front of the mirror wearing a sexy silk outfit, with Max's pearls around her neck, rouging her cheeks, when she heard a knock at the door.

Before she could answer, Johnny burst into the room.

'All right,' he shouted. 'You wanna tell me about it?'

Giselle continued rouging her cheeks. 'You're a smart boy,' she said coolly. 'You figure it out.'

'Tell me!' Johnny hissed.

Giselle turned from the mirror and crossed her legs, letting the silk skirt fall open at the slit.

'Let's just say I was protecting my interests . . '

Johnny looked at her. 'What interests?'

Giselle's cool façade fell away. 'You know what you get for being "Miss Subways"?' she shouted, jumping up and pacing around the room. 'Nothing! *Rien*! Not even a free ride on the uptown express!'

She touched her pearls tenderly.

'I have other things in mind!'

Johnny shook his head. 'Max is not stupid!' Johnny said.

'Ah,' Giselle laughed, 'but he *is* in love.'

Johnny shook his head. 'You are something else, lady.'

'One day you will grow up, Johnny Castle, and not take matters of the heart so seriously.'

Johnny took a deep breath and walked to the

door. He put his hand on the doorknob, turned and stared at her.

'I hope that day never comes,' he said. He stared at her a moment longer, enraged and walked out the door, slamming it shut behind him.

Ten

The hotel bar was empty except for two young couples in the corner drinking pina coladas, when Max walked in. He sat at the bar next to Sweets who was talking quietly to Harry, the bartender.

'Gimma a bourbon,' Max said, without a greeting.

'What're you talking about?' Harry said. 'You never touch the stuff!'

Max glared. His eyes dark and angry. 'I said gimme a bourbon,' he ordered.

The bartender slid the drink down the bar, but before Max could drink it, Johnny stormed into the room and darted over to him.

'I know you fired me. I just want to tell you – I never touched her. And that's the truth!' Johnny turned and stalked out. Max looked after him, his drink in mid-air, his mouth open.

He put the bourbon glass down and walked over to Sweets.

'That no-good . . . I've had my eye on him before. That business with Baby and all, but I *never* thought that kid would play dirty with me,' Max said, his face enraged.

'Hey, Max, cool it,' Sweets said.

'I'll be glad to get rid of him. Who needs him here anyway?'

'Hold it, boss!' Sweets said. 'First of all, *you* do. Everyone likes Johnny. He's a great dancer and teacher. The ladies like him and he's a decent, hardworking kid trying to make his life better.'

Max shook his head, calming down a bit under the influence of Sweets' soothing voice.

'I don't know. I told him she was my girl. I even had him teach me the cha-cha in confidence so I could impress her. And he promised he wouldn't tell anyone.'

'Did he?' Sweets asked.

Max shook his head. 'No,' he admitted, his face easing up slowly. 'No, he didn't.'

'Listen Max,' Sweets said. 'Sometimes you gotta look at both sides of a situation. Look at the source of the story as well as the so-called villain.'

'What do you mean?' Max asked angrily.

'Are you suggesting that Giselle . . . ?'

Sweets raised his eyebrows and shrugged. 'She's your lady, Max. You know her best.'

'Sweets, tell me something.'

'Anything, Max. Shoot.'

'You know Johnny. He ever promise something . . . then go back on his word?'

Sweet swiveled on the bar stool and looked Max straight in the eye.

'I'll tell you,' Sweets said, slow and easy. 'Johnny can be a lotta things. He can be a pain in the neck. He can drive a person crazy. But one thing he doesn't do – never – is go back on his word. Where Johnny comes from, that's all he's got. Honesty.'

Max shook his head.

'Thanks, Sweets.' He left the drink and walked out of the bar.

Giselle was back at the mirror admiring herself, fondling her pearls slowly when Max stormed in without knocking.

'Finally, Max!' Giselle cooed, smiling. 'I have been waiting.'

She got up and walked over to Max, caressing his cheek.

'You look . . . worried,' Giselle said, hesitantly, stroking his hair.

'I am,' Max replied coldly, removing her hand from his head.

'I don't like being lied to.'

'Vat are you talking about?' Giselle asked,

using her best Belgian accent.

'Giselle, I can sleep a long time, you know, but eventually the alarm clock goes off.'

Giselle looked puzzled. 'I am not familiar with . . . '

'You're wrong,' Max interrupted. 'I'm the one who's not familiar with . . . women like you.'

He chuckled as he watched the expression on her face change.

'I guess you thought I was a rich guy, with this place and all. Well, you can go home easy. I'm in hock up to my eyeballs.'

Giselle coughed, taken aback by his admission. 'I did not know . . . '

Max smiled. 'We both have a lot to learn. But don't worry about me, honey. I'm a little bruised, but I'll mend.'

'Max . . . ' Giselle said.

'I'll have your bags picked up in an hour,' Max said, cutting her off. 'And leave the pearls at the desk.'

Max turned and walked out of the room.

He headed down the steps and directly over to the staff dance room.

Inside, Johnny was alone, collecting some records. His eyes were dark and moody as he moved absent-mindedly to the beat of a tune blasting loudly on the juke box.

He was startled when Max walked in.

'I'm glad I found you,' Max said. 'I thought maybe you'd . . .'

'Don't worry I'm outta here,' Johnny interrupted as he turned off the music. 'I was just getting some things.'

'You're not going anywhere,' Max said.

'Look, this day hasn't made a lotta sense so far, but I thought I was tired,' Johnny said, putting down a stack of 45s.

'Why should you be?' Max smiled. 'You didn't do anything wrong, did you?'

'Uh . . . no.'

'Good. At least I got one thing right this week.' Max hesitated, embarrassed. 'Could you . . . you know . . . tell me . . . what *did* happen?'

Johnny looked awkwardly at his feet.

'Well, she . . .'

He trailed off uncomfortably while Max waited.

'Seduced you?'

'Tried to, anyway,' Johnny said, shrugging.

'Tried to?' Max asked dubiously. 'Johnny . . . this is Max you're talking to.'

'Max, I'm telling you, she came into my room, took off her clothes and . . .'

Max broke in. 'Thanks. I can fill in the rest myself.'

'No! No!' Johnny shouted. 'Nothing happened. I told her to leave.'

Max looked at Johnny, considering the ex-
planation.

'She just came in . . . and took her clothes
off?' Max repeated.

'That's about it,' Johnny said.

'Has that ever happened to you before?' Max
asked Johnny, man to man.

'No.'

'Me neither,'

'Maybe that's the way they do it in Belgium,'
Johnny said.

Max nodded in agreement. 'That must be it.'
He paused a moment. 'She just came in, huh?
While you were sleeping?'

'Just walked right in the door,' Johnny said. 'I
didn't even hear it.'

'Uh, how did you—' Max hesitated. 'You
know, how did you resist?'

'She was your woman,' Johnny said matter-of-
factly.

'Very good,' Max nodded. 'Very honorable.
So, how did you resist?'

Johnny sighed and shook his head. 'I have
absolutely no idea.'

Max sat on the stage, fascinated by the scen-
ario. 'So what you're saying is . . . she just

walked in the door and . . . ' He stopped himself and looked at Johnny.

'Never mind. Haven't you got a job you should
be doing here?'

Johnny smiled, flashing his gorgeous white
teeth and blue eyes.

'I sure do, Max. And thanks.'

Max returned the smile and walked out of the
dance room.

Later that day, Max ambled into the ballroom
and perched on a window seat, staring out at the
beautiful blue sky, tall evergreens and pines and
colorful flowers, lost in thought. Baby walked
up and sat down next to him.

'Are you all right, Dad?' she asked.

Max shook his head and gave her a small
smile. 'I was a fool . . . ' he started.

'So was I,' Baby added. He turned from the
window and looked at her.

'You're just trying to make me feel better,
right?'

'Yeah!' she smiled.

'I love you for it,' he said, taking her hand. He
pulled her close for a warm, fatherly hug.

Later that night, Baby and Johnny walked across
the bridge to the staff dance room. They stood

outside on the porch listening to the music for a
while. Inside, the staff was dancing to a loud,
fast song, hopping and popping, slinking and
swaying to the beat.

Johnny led Baby to the door to go inside.

'I still can't . . . I mean . . . I *hit* you!' she
cried.

'Forget it,' Johnny shrugged.

'I *can't* forget it,' Baby shook her head.

'It's nothin',' Johnny said.

'You make it sound like it happens everyday,'
she smiled.

'Well, it's not the first time!' he laughed.

'Really?' Baby looked incredulous.

'No way,' Johnny said.

'So,' Baby said, intrigued by his admission,
'tell me about the others.'

'They hit harder!'

'Hey!' Baby laughed. 'I hit you pretty good!'

'Not like they did.'

'They must have had pretty good reasons,
huh?' she asked.

Johnny shrugged again. 'Pretty good.'

'Like?' she pressed.

He looked at her for a long moment, then
broke out laughing and dragged her into the
dance.

*   *   *

Out on the grounds, Max Kellerman reviewed the past few days in his mind, feeling like a fool.

'No fool like an old fool,' he said out loud.

He stopped suddenly as he heard the music coming from the staff quarters. He listened a moment and smiled.

' . . .*four*, five six, *four*, five six,' he said out loud as he did a little dance step, smiling to himself.

'At least it wasn't a total loss,' he chuckled, as he cha-chaed across the lawn. 'Next time I'll be ready for the dance!'

Don't miss . . .

Book Two

HELLO, STRANGER

Turn over the page for a sneak preview!

HELLO, STRANGER

Kellerman's looked pretty as a postcard in the summer sun. A postcard in which everything was perfect. The pool. The tennis courts. The croquet field. The three-legged race on the lawn. A postcard in which everyone was smiling and having a good time. Except Baby. Baby, unsmiling, was clearly not having a good time. She was pacing back and forth by the side entrance of Kellerman's. Back and forth. Back and forth. Every few turns she would stop for a second, stare down the drive, sigh. Then she would start pacing again.

Norman's eyes followed her. He looked like he was watching a tennis match. 'But what do you think, Baby?' he asked the back of her head. 'Do you think it is just a rumor? 'Cause if it is just a rumor, then there's no sense in me getting myself all worked up about it, is there? I mean, if Harry Ballantine's not coming to the Catskills, I can relax, right? I don't have to come up with any new jokes about my father. On the other hand,' he continued, this time to her face as she marched towards him, 'if Harry Ballantine is going to be in the Catskills, I'd be a fool not to be prepared, right? I mean, this could be my big break. Harry Ballantine, Mr Broadway. My once in a lifetime. Right, Baby? Don't you think so? Don't you think if Harry Ballan—'

Baby came to a sudden stop in front of him. 'Norman!' she almost shouted. 'Enough is enough already, okay? Right now I am interested in only one person who is coming to the Catskills, and it isn't Harry Ballantine. It is Elizabeth Kellerman. My mother. Have you got that?'

Norman looked crestfallen. 'Yeah, sure, Baby. I mean, yeah, I know your mother's coming. I was just trying—'

'Yes,' snapped Baby. 'You *are* trying. So just stop it, okay?'

Norman opened his mouth to say something more, but at that moment Robin rushed up. She was wearing a Kelly-green sun dress with white polka dots. 'Well,' she giggled, twirling in front of them, 'how do I look?'

'You look like a golf course,' said Norman, his good mood beginning to return.

Robin made a face. 'Gimme a break, Norm, will ya? I lost three pounds this week, just by simple starvation.'

Norman smiled. 'Okay. You look like a miniature golf course.'

Robin punched his arm. 'You better watch out, Norman. If you're not careful, you might accidentally get funny.'

Baby threw up her hands in despair. 'Come on, you two, cut it out, will you? This is no time to be fooling around. This is serious. My mother's going to be here any minute.'

Robin shrugged. 'So? What's the big deal? She's not Bobby Vinton. She's only your mother. You've met her before.'

Baby groaned. 'Robin, for Pete's sake. She and my father have barely said ten words to each other since they split up—'

'And I bet six of them can't be used in polite conversation,' cut in Norman.

Baby ignored him. 'And now she's coming up here. In person. The woman who said Kellerman's wasn't big enough for the both of them.' She waited for a second to let this sink in. 'What am I supposed to do, huh? How am I supposed to handle this? If it weren't for me coming here this summer she'd still be at home. Playing bridge.'

'Oh come on, Baby,' Robin soothed, 'it's her birthday tomorrow. They've gotta be nice to each other, right? And she'll be in a good mood. Everything'll be fine.'

Baby took a deep breath. 'Robin, try to pay attention, will you? My mother is going to be forty-six years old tomorrow. That's practically fifty. Her life is in tatters. You have no idea what it's been like for her, my father leaving like that. She cried for months. And when she stopped crying she started eating. I'd find her in the kitchen at one in the morning, watching a late

movie on the portable TV and demolishing a
chocolate cake single-handed. There wasn't anything in the refrigerator that was safe from her.'
Baby looked from Robin to Norman. 'My mother
is this old, divorced, overweight woman. Do
you think she's going to be happy it's her
birthday? Do you think she's going to be beside
herself with joy to come up here and see how
well my father's doing, surrounded by all these
rich, attractive women?'

Robin put her hand on her shoulder. 'Look,
Baby, it's been a few years now. Your mother's
bound to be over the worst.' She turned to
Norman. 'Right, Norm?'

Norman nodded in agreement.

'That's what you think,' said Baby. 'You don't
know my mother. She was born to be a housewife. The family was everything to her.'

Suddenly their conversation was drowned out
by the sound of Peter, Paul and Mary singing 'If
I Had a Hammer' blaring from a car radio.

Norman whistled. 'Wow, nice car.' A brand
new red sports car came tearing up the drive.
The woman at the wheel, singing along to the
music, blasted the horn as the car squealed to a
stop in front of the entrance.

'Nice lady, too,' said Norman as an extremely
attractive woman in tight jeans, boots and a
bright pink silk shirt stepped out.

She slammed the door behind her and started
up the stairs, smiling at them brightly. Norman

smiled back. Several male guests who were passing by smiled back too.

'What's so familiar about her?' Robin whispered to Baby.

Baby shrugged. 'I'm not sure.'

And then Robin's jaw dropped. 'Oh my God!' she gasped as the stranger reached the porch. 'Aunt Lizzie!'

Baby paled. 'Mom?' she croaked. 'Mom?'

'Baby!' Elizabeth rushed up and threw her arms around her daughter. 'Oh, Baby! Let me look at you!' she said, taking a step back, but not letting go. 'It's so good to see you.'

Speechless, Norman and Robin just stood there staring.

'Mom?' Baby repeated, pretty speechless herself.

But Elizabeth was too happy to see the effect she was having. 'How are you, honey? You look wonderful. Absolutely wonderful.'

Baby cleared her throat. 'You look . . . you um . . . where'd you get the car?'

'You like it? You can take it for a spin later if you want. It was my birthday present to myself. After all,' she beamed, 'it isn't every day a woman reaches the prime of her life, is it?'

'The prime of . . . ' whispered Baby, unable to take her eyes off her mother. 'But you . . . what have you done to yourself?'

Elizabeth did a little turn. 'What do you think? I was always really a ten, you know,' she said, winking at the girls. 'Under my size fourteen, that is.'

Robin giggled appreciatively.

Baby threw her a dark look. 'But, Mom, your hair. Your hair wasn't that color before.'

Elizabeth laughed, shaking her head so that the curls bounced. 'It's pretty good, isn't it? I have this new hairdresser in Manhattan—'

'Manhattan!' Baby was looking at her mother as though she had lost her mind. 'You go all the way to Manhattan to have your hair done?'

'Well, not exactly,' said Elizabeth, taking a breath. 'He's actually right around the corner from my new apartment.'

'Your new what?'

Elizabeth's smile lost a little of its sparkle. 'My new apartment. I—'

'What are you talking about, your new apartment? What happened to our house?'

Elizabeth put her arm around her. 'Let's go somewhere where we can sit down and talk, shall we, and I'll tell you all about it.' She started down the stairs. Baby reached out and grabbed Robin's hand, pulling her with them.

Not even Elizabeth seemed eager to sit in the confined space of a room, so they decided to go and sit by the pool. At least they couldn't actually get into a fight out there in the open, surrounded by scores of sun-soaked guests and their shrieking children.

Elizabeth sat down across from Baby and Robin. 'I don't know,' she said, her eyes circling the pool. 'Do you think there were always this many fat men up here or did I just not notice? Look at them. They look like beached whales.'

'Oh, Aunt Lizzie . . . ' laughed Robin.

Baby poked her in the ribs. 'Mom, I thought we were going to talk about you.'

Elizabeth was rummaging for something in her bag. 'We are, honey, I just have to find—' She pulled out a six-month supply of tissues, a make-up bag, several sets of keys, a notebook, a flashlight, and a spark-plug. 'Now where . . . I know it's in here somewhere . . . '

Neil sauntered by, on his way to the lifeguard station. 'Hey, there, Baby,' he said, with what Baby and Robin had nicknamed his 'I am God's gift to college girls' grin. He stopped for a second to take in Elizabeth. 'Who's your friend?'

Baby scowled. 'She's not my—'

'Aren't you going to introduce us?'

Baby sighed. 'Mom, this is Neil. Neil, this is my mother.' Elizabeth looked up and returned Neil's smile. 'Neil would love to stay and talk but, sadly, he has a job to do. Don't you, Neil?'

'Sure thing.' Neil winked at Baby. 'Catch you later. Nice to meet you, Mrs Kellerman.'

'Oh yes,' said Elizabeth vaguely, her attention back in the depths of her bag, 'nice to meet you too. Ah!' She looked up triumphantly, bringing a book into the sunlight. 'Here it is!' She handed it

to Baby. 'I brought this for you, honey. This is
the book that changed my life. Once you've read
this book, you'll understand exactly what's happened to me.'

Baby and Robin stared at the book in Baby's
hands. *The Feminine Mystique,*' they read together.

'Hey,' said Robin. 'I've heard of this book. Isn't
it the one that says sex is good and women should
just go out and get it, just like men do?'

'Robin!' gasped Baby, putting the book
between them on the lounger. 'Well,' she said
primly, turning to her mother, '*I* never heard
of it.'

Elizabeth reached over and took the book
back. 'Well, you should have. It should be
required reading for every woman. They should
give you a copy with your first box of sanitary
napkins.'

Robin giggled.

'Mom!' First Baby hadn't been able to believe
her eyes. Now she couldn't believe her ears.
Was this *her* mother? The mother who had run
the bake sale every year for the PTA? The
mother who had been the leader of Girl Scout
Troop 517 for six years? The mother who was the
bridge champion of Roslyn, Long Island? 'Mom,
I don't understand—'

'You will, honey, you will. Listen to this.'
Elizabeth opened the book to a page she had
marked. ' "Perhaps it is only a sick or immature

society that chooses to make women house-
wives, not people."' She looked up expectantly.
'Well, what do you think of that?'

Robin was wide-eyed. 'You mean you're sick
if you're a housewife? Wow. You know, I always
thought that myself, but I was afraid to say anything.' She frowned thoughtfully. 'Aunt Lizzie,
do you think it makes any difference if you've
got a maid?'

'But, Mom,' broke in Baby, 'you spent the last
twenty years of your life being a housewife!'

Elizabeth nodded victoriously. 'Exactly!'

Max and Sweets were walking down the patio
steps, heading towards the pool, deep in conversation. Max shrugged wearily. 'I don't know,'
he was saying, 'I must need my head examined.
It's the stupidest thing I've done since I hired
Johnny. I ask you, whatever possessed me to
invite her up here for her birthday? My ex-wife.
I'm nuts, that's what I am. I'm beginning to
show the strain.'

Sweets grinned. 'You said it broke your heart
to think of her sitting in that big empty house all
by herself on her birthday.'

'Did I?'

'Yup. That's what you said.' Sweets touched
him on the arm. 'Your heart was in the right
place.'

Max gave a choked little laugh. 'Even if my

brain wasn't.' He spread his hands in a gesture
of helplessness. 'It's just that she's going to look
at me with those big, sad eyes of hers. You don't
know what it does to me, Sweets. The guilt. She
looks at me like every bad thing that ever happened in the world is my fault. Everything.
World War Two. The starving children in India.
The Ku Klux Klan . . . ' Suddenly he brightened. 'Wait a minute, wait a minute,' he said,
becoming excited. 'I have an idea. We'll tell Baby
we have to go into town. Pick out a new pedal
for the piano. That's bound to take up most of
the afternoon. Maybe the whole afternoon.
Maybe—'

Sweets was looking at him skeptically. 'Max,
you can't spend the whole time she's up here
buying a piano pedal.'

'You've got to back me up on this, Sweets. I'm
your friend, remember that.'

'Come on, man . . . '

'Okay, forget that. I sign your paychecks.
Remember that.'

'Max . . . ' laughed Sweets.

Max grabbed his arm. 'Look. There's Baby and
Robin over by the pool with one of the guests.
Come on, let's tell her.'

'Max, I . . . ' Sweets began, but Max was
already striding away.

Max was in such a state of agitation that,
coming up behind Elizabeth, he didn't so much

as glance at her. 'Honey,' he said to Baby, talking quickly, 'honey, I'm afraid something's come up.'

Both girls were staring at him in an odd way, but he didn't notice that either.

'Dad,' smiled Baby, 'look who's—'

'I'm really sorry about this, honey. Really. But the pedal on the piano—' He tugged Sweets forward. 'Sweets, tell her about the piano pedal.'

'Your father's a big chicken. He wants to make himself scarce so he doesn't have to see you-know-who.'

Robin winced, covering her mouth to hide the smile she couldn't quite control.

'Dad!' Baby's voice held a clear warning. 'Dad—'

But it was a warning Max wasn't going to pay any attention to. Just as he wasn't going to pay any attention to the fact that the odd way they'd been looking at him had turned to one of horror. 'All right,' he said, standing so close to Elizabeth that his hand brushed the back of her chair. 'All right. I'm avoiding your mother.'

Robin buried her face in her hands.

Baby tried to motion with her eyes. 'Dad—'

'I admit that. I *am* avoiding her. But you would, too, if you were me. She's just going to make me feel guilty and miserable like she always does. You don't know what it's like—'

All of a sudden the woman who had been

sitting in front of him, the woman he hadn't so much as glanced at, was standing up and turning around. She was speaking. To him.

'Oh, but I do know, Max,' she was saying, 'I know exactly what it's like.'

For a few seconds, Max couldn't figure out who she was. He knew she was familiar, but from where?

'Don't worry, Max,' she smiled at him, 'you don't have to feel that way any more. Really. I'm fine now. I'm better than I've been in years.'

'Lizzie?' he said faintly.

She turned her new 100-watt smile in another direction. 'Nice to see you, Sweets.'

Sweets grinned broadly. 'Likewise, Mrs K. You're lookin' good.' He took hold of her hand. 'Real good.'

Max was coming back to life. 'You're looking . . . ' He was unable to take his eyes off her. 'You're. . . Lizzie, have you lost your mind?'

Elizabeth Kellerman, wife, mother, and carpool organizer, laughed. 'No, Max, no, I haven't lost my mind. I've found it. It's been in the deep freeze for the last twenty years, but now I've got it back.'

Max's eyes went from her hair to her shirt to her figure-hugging jeans to her polished leather boots. 'Well,' he spluttered, 'if this is any indication of what the defrosting has done, my advice to you would be to set the temperature back down.'

The smile vanished from her face. 'I should've known,' she said coolly. 'Just like always. The same old Max. Still trying to control me. Still part of the male establishment.'

The male establishment? What was she talking about? 'At least I act my age,' Max spluttered. 'At least I know my place.'

'Dad,' interrupted Baby, not knowing whether she wanted to stop the argument or heat it up. 'Dad, Mom was just going to tell us about her new apartment.'

'In Manhattan,' Robin chipped in helpfully.

'What?'

Elizabeth's smile came back. 'Right around the corner from Bleecker Street.' She turned to Sweets. 'You know, where all those great jazz clubs are.'

'Smart lady,' said Sweets. 'That's a great neighborhood.'

Max didn't look like he thought it was such a great neighborhood.

'And,' continued Elizabeth, sounding like someone who had saved the best part for last, 'it's just a few blocks from NYU. Where I'll be going to college in the fall.'

'College?' gasped Baby.

Robin gaped at her aunt in admiration. 'Wow.'

Elizabeth put her arm around her daughter. 'We'll both be freshmen, honey. Isn't that exciting?'

Baby blinked. 'Mom—'

'Wait a minute,' broke in Max. 'What have you done with the house, Lizzie? Where's my house?'

'Right on the corner of Kenwood Drive, where you left it. I've already had a few offers for it though. After I've unpacked we can go over them.' She gave Baby a little hug. 'Want to show me to my room now, honey?'

'You're doing this to get back at me, aren't you, Lizzie?' Max called as she and Baby started walking away. 'It's revenge, that's what it is.'

Elizabeth stopped and faced him. 'I'm doing this for me, Max, not for you. I've stopped thinking "divorced" and started thinking "single". I'm going to enjoy myself now,' she said, turning on her heel. 'Just like you.'

'Boy,' sighed Robin, gazing after them.

'That's some lady,' said Sweets.

Max jammed his hands into his pockets. 'How'd she get her hair like that?'

We hope you enjoyed reading this book. If you would like to receive further information about titles available in the Bantam series, just write to the address below, with your name and address: Kim Prior, Bantam Books, 61-63 Uxbridge Road, Ealing, London W5 5SA.

If you live in Australia or New Zealand and would like more information about the series, please write to:

Sally Porter	Kiri Martin
Transworld Publishers	Transworld Publishers (NZ) Ltd
(Australia) Pty Ltd.	Cnr. Moselle and Waipareira
15-23 Helles Avenue	Avenues
Moorebank	Henderson
N.S.W. 2170	Auckland
AUSTRALIA	NEW ZEALAND

All Bantam Young Adult books are available at your bookshop or newsagent, or can be ordered from the following address: Corgi/Bantam Books, Cash Sales Department, PO Box 11, Falmouth, Cornwall. TR10 9EN.

Please list the title(s) you would like, and send together with a cheque or postal order. You should allow for the cost of the book(s) plus postage and packing charges as follows:

All orders up to a total of £5.00: 50p
All orders in excess of £5.00: Free

Please note that payment must be made in pounds sterling: other currencies are unacceptable.

(The above applies to readers in the UK and Republic of Ireland only)

B.F.P.O. customers, please allow for the cost of the book(s) plus the following for postage and packing: 60p for the first book, 25p for the second book and 15p per copy for the next 7 books, thereafter 9p per book.

Overseas customers, please allow £1.25 for postage and packing for the first book, 75p for the second book, and 28p for each subsequent title ordered.

It's hot! It's sexy! It's fun!

Baby's life changes forever when she meets Johnny. For he is an electrifying dancer, and he shows Baby what dancing is *really* all about – the heat, the rhythm and the excitement . . .

A sensational series based on the characters from the top-grossing *Dirty Dancing* movie and television series.

Available now:

1. BABY, IT'S YOU
2. HELLO, STRANGER

Coming soon:

3. SAVE THE LAST DANCE FOR ME
4. BREAKING UP IS HARD TO DO
5. STAND BY ME
6. OUR DAY WILL COME